AF421934

Romero: Hollywood Fixer

By

Edwin Betancourt Jr.

Chapter 1

It's 8:10 A.M.

Today is January 8, 2023.

I've been staring at the calendar on my desk for the last ten minutes. I've scribbled an X in red marker on the date January 20th...God, how I loathe that date.

I placed the marker down and stared at the client who'd been in my office for the past five minutes, praying his troubles would go away.

Seated in front of my desk was five-time Grammy Award winning rapper Lil Yeller, aka Marcus Payne.

Marcus has had an amazing career for the last six years, all thanks to his management team. He had sponsorship deals from trendy clothing brands and occasional opportunities to write theme songs for television shows and commercials.

Unfortunately, Marcus decided to do something completely idiotic, leaving his career and everything he had worked hard for, hanging in limbo.

When Marcus called me last night, I expected him to come into my office the next day with a lot to say. It's been five minutes of silence; the only noise filling up my office are the car horns outside of my three-story office building.

"Look, Marcus." I began finally breaking the silence, as I was no longer drawing Xs all over anything that had January 20th on it. "I can't help you if you won't at least tell me what went through your mind, when you decided to post that picture for your eight and a half million Twitter followers to see."

Marcus Payne reminded me of Eminem, well, a less talented version of him. He was in his early thirties, Caucasian with short blond hair and blue eyes.

Huh, I wonder if that's what his label was going for when they signed him.

The rapper seated before me wore two sets of gold chains around his neck, no one understood why, not even him. Record labels felt every rapper should wear golden chains around their necks because it shows importance.

I've never been into rap music because a majority of the songs tend to be homophobic. As a gay man, hearing those lyrics was insulting. And the ironic part? I know about eighty percent of the male rappers are actually closeted! Hearing those lyrics come out of their mouths is comically sad. It honestly wasn't surprising because these rappers all have personas and reputations to protect.

Lil Yeller was no different. Not only is he a White rapper that claims he was born in the South Bronx and faced troubling obstacles, but he created a tough and headstrong facade in the industry that had struck fear in the hearts of his doubters. Unfortunately, that man in question was now shaken up and too nervous to speak, kind of ironic for a rapper named Yeller.

"Aight, so listen."

I glared at him and he quickly stopped speaking. He cleared his throat and continued, changing his demeanor from a tough guy to a mature and civilized adult, sounding like the Harvard graduate that the world doesn't actually know he is!

"Alright, so it all began when President Elect Victor Reber won the damn election. I mean, who the hell votes for a racist?"

"So instead of tweeting from a fake profile like everyone else does, you decide to take a picture of you shoving your penis into a blow-up doll's mouth with the president's face edited on it?"

Marcus nodded his head, "Yeah, I did! It's what anyone else would've done. Why do I get singled out for it?"

That question wasn't one that needed to be justified verbally. It needed to be shown to the clueless rapper.

I grabbed the remote control off my desk, pressed the 'Power On' button and within seconds the plasma television screen which was mounted on the wall behind me, turned on and Marcus' demeanor once again changed. This time he had regret written all over his face.

"According to multiple reports, rapper Lil Yeller wasn't too thrilled with the idea of a Republican finally leading this amazing country. The loud liberal was so upset that he uploaded a cruel and sexually explicit picture of himself doing something unthinkable to a sex doll with the president's face edited on it and posted it online, showing Americans just how much of a traitor he really is! Is this the type of artist you want to support, America? Is this the type of man you want your children looking up to? A man who hates this amazing and glorious country, that his only form of protest is to violate a blow-up doll? No! I know I will no longer be supporting this man or his music any longer."

The annoying and squeaky voice filling my eardrums belonged to Republican mouthpiece Tani Tane. A woman who will do anything to get on top. She bashes and labels anyone against Victor Reber as a traitor.

But if you were hiding deadly secrets from your past, like she is, then you too would do whatever it takes to make sure you please the right people in the right places. Republicans who own her network television show are now the ones who own her.

I quickly muted the television, not wanting to hear another word that came out of her mouth, for my own sanity.

"I'm a traitor?! Is she serious? All I did was pretend to screw a blow-up doll! I didn't kill anyone. Surely you can do something about this."

"Well hell! Did you forget who I am? I'm Jayson Romero. I am the Hollywood Fixer after all. Meaning people like you who are dealing with things like this, aka a crisis, come to me and I fix it. All I care about is your image, that's it. Anything else falls solely on you and your team. I'm here to make sure you pop out of this crap storm unscathed."

The rapper shook his head. "I screwed up."

"No, screwing up would be getting a groupie pregnant because you stupidly forgot to put on a condom. What you did was just protest the president in a very weird way that I'm sure is going to get you new and perverted followers. No biggy."

"No biggy?" Marcus let out a nervous chuckle, "Bro, I lost seven million Twitter followers. All my deals have been dropped. Sneakers, movies, cartoons, hell, even ShowToyz isn't going to make me an action figure anymore!"

I nodded, calmly listening to his rant.

When his record label hired me to take this on, I was skeptical at first, but seeing the passion in the blue eyes of this Eminem knock off, I could tell his career was important to him.

"I understand how scary this must be for you. Me? This isn't my first walk in the park. I've done this many times before."

"What?" Marcus gasped, looking at me up and down. "You look like you're twenty!"

"Awww, thank you!"

I have been told I look young by many people and that compliment was always one that made me blush. In reality, I'm twenty-nine years old and in the gay world that's about ninety- nine. Once I turn thirty, the gay world will legally declare me old and dead.

But many of my enemies know that even though I look young and have a voice which outs me whenever I speak, that I kick ass at my job and my bite is far worse than my bark!

Knock! Knock!

The knocking on my office door caused Marcus to flinch. I smirked, shaking my head. "Come in!" I shouted.

The door opened, and standing in the doorway was my assistant, Anthony Santos.

Anthony is a 5'10" Hispanic man who is notorious for wearing custom fitted designer suits. He has caramel colored skin and dark brown curly hair that tends to be left in a small afro. He has a pair of light brown eyes that everyone compliments whenever they walk into my office. His clean-shaven face and sharp jawline makes him look more like an innocent GQ model than my assistant.

An innocent and naïve face that makes it easier to hide the darkness which lurks within him.

"I got the pictures you asked for." Anthony said, showing me the manila envelope he was holding in his hands.

"Oh, that's perfect! How did they come out?"

Anthony nodded with a smile on his face. "Perfect! Better than any of us could have anticipated."

"And did you take care of the written response I sent you this morning?"

Anthony once again nodded, entering the office and handed me the envelope. "It didn't need much revising so it'll be live in a couple of seconds."

I took the envelope from him and smiled widely. "Oooh, I cannot wait! Thank you so much!"

Anthony waved at Marcus and he exited the office, closing the door behind him.

Poor Marcus probably had no idea what my assistant and I were talking about, as he stared blankly at me.

"Do you remember Dave Alex, the former mayor of Singler City?" I asked, which caused the rapper to immediately shake his head.

"While Dave Alex was running for mayor, he painted this beautiful image of his family life; wife, kids and white picket fences. You know the same old cliché bull crap closeted politicians use to get votes with. Well, I knew Dave from my college days and he was in a very long relationship with a guy from my public relations class. Anyway, he was caught on a hot mic a few months after being elected, where he referred to gays as—and I quote—Cancerous beings who need to be sedated or eradicated."

Marcus shook his head again, probably this time in disgust. "That's sick. Why would he say that?"

"He was surrounded by male politicians who view the gay community as such and instead of defending the same community he is secretly a part of; he decided to bash us to gain brownie points with the jocks."

Men like Dave have always frustrated me. The closeted gay/bi/pansexual men who unleash their inner homophobia on gay men because they're too weak to stand out from the crowd. Men like that are sick and disgusting. Vile and hypocritical.

Unfortunately, that's the world we live in. A world where people who want to seem cool jump on a bandwagon to bash marginalized people. Men who do that aren't men at all, they're just scared little boys.

"But of course, he blamed that comment on the Ambien he took the night before and all was forgiven. Considering I knew him, he wasn't on Ambien. Nor was that something he said by accident. But no one said or did a thing. It was labeled 'locker room talk' and forgotten by everyone including the media, the next day...well, everyone except me. Anthony is very gifted with an ability to manipulate photos."

"You mean like Photoshop?" the rapper asked.

I nodded. "In a way, yes. But the program he uses is a bit more advanced; because it shows no traces of manipulation should the FBI, or anyone else, analyze it."

I leaned my back on the chair and continued with my story, getting to the good part, "Someone accidentally leaked a photo of dear old Mayor Alex in a very compromising position and that position was him partaking in some illegal narcotics."

"Wait! You leaked manipulated images of the mayor? That's illegal. That's wrong. That's—"

"Genius, I know. I could've gone another route, but one thing about me is that I don't out people. Never have and never will." I smiled, proud of my accomplishments and the boundaries I've set.

"I'm getting to your thing in a minute." I replied just in case the rapper was trying to find the relevancy in my long-winded speech. "Anyway, once those images leaked, the mayor was impeached and his wife forced him into a rehab clinic. Now, I know the story seems bad but he was photographed two years ago at Coachella tonguing down some Twink, so I'd say he's doing quite well for himself."

My laughter was probably a little extreme in the aftermath of the story I just told, but I needed it to highlight everything I'm capable of.

"Okay, but what does this have to do with me again?"

I unclasped the manila envelope and took out a picture. I looked at the picture and continued smiling at the amazing job Anthony had done.

The picture currently circulating the internet is of Lil Yeller nude with his penis inside of the mouth of a sex doll and stupidly sticking his tongue out while giving a thumbs up. But the picture in my hand didn't have him nude and with a sex doll. Instead, he was standing on the sandy beach wearing shorts and holding a pool noodle over his crotch, similar to the playful way most immature frat boys do for no reason. And on his right breast is a tattoo of the Aries zodiac symbol.

Nothing besides the item, lighting and clothes changed in the picture. His smile was the same as the original as well as his position. It was an eerily similar picture in every way.

Now I know how weight loss corporations feel when they manipulate photos revealing fake results.

"Okay, since your photo went viral, every media outlet has knocked down anything stupid the president tweeted and has made your mishap their breaking news. But here is the original photo we're going to say was manipulated."

I handed the picture over to Lil Yeller and his eyes widened. His eyes were such a nice shade of blue.

"Are you kidding me? I don't even have a tattoo!"

"Yeah, about that. I booked you for an appointment in an hour at The Forbidden Ones Ink Shop. Davey is going to give you the temporary airbrush tattoo."

"What? No one is going to believe that!"

"Why not? You never take your shirt off and up until this stupid photo fiasco you never posted any shirtless pictures. Trust me, no one even knows you have nipples."

He stopped talking and sighed, probably realizing he doesn't have much of a choice in this situation. "So, you're just gonna leak this pic?"

"Not quite. Before you stepped into my office, I already came up with a very lengthy response as well as the details of this photo. In a few minutes, it's going to go live. But before it does, I'm going to need you to read it, so you can get a better understanding of the lie you're going to tell TMZ when they stalk you at the airport."

I dug my hand back inside of the envelope and took out a piece of paper, I handed it to the rapper and he took it, probably confused about what I was giving him.

"Please go on and read it." I said, the happy-yet sinister smile still plastered on my face.

The rapper nodded his head and he began to read the letter aloud,

"Yo! These r crazy times so let me get real with u! I dunno what that pic is of me and that sex doll. First things first, I don't play that way! Not to mention I have a tattoo on my right chest that clearly ain't in the photo. I'm being set up by someone! It's mad sad that y'all think that photo is actually me. Probably them trolls who found out President Reber wanted me to perform at the inauguration. But don't be mad, I got the FBI looking into this!—" Marcus stopped reading and looked at me. "The FBI? Wouldn't they deny this claim?"

"They could." I responded back. "But let's just say the director of the FBI owes me a favor for a pro-bono job I did for him a few months back."

Marcus stared at me for a few seconds and then he decided to continue reading,

"I kno how crazy this looks but I ain't playing around. My fans kno I ain't about that disrespectful shiz! Y'all kno how I feel about this country and how I feel about nudity. But here ya'll go! I'm gonna post the real pic of me, I ain't happy with the people who hacked my phone, took that pic and Photoshopped it to start with. Here's the real pic. I kno y'all are mad, shiz, I'm mad too! But don't worry, we'll get thru this together. Peace and love, Lil Yeller!"

Marcus finished reading the letter and he stared at it in silence. "This sounds exactly like something I would say!"

I proudly nodded my head. "Duh! I don't care much for your music, but I studied that fake and racist accent you put on during your interviews and I decided to just roll with it."

Ding!

Ding!

Ding!

Ding!

Ding!

Marcus quickly took his cellphone out of his jeans' pocket and was met with various notifications. He swiped up and down the screen in excitement. "Holy crap! The post worked! I'm getting apologies from various people and even the network that took my theme song off! I'm in the clear!"

"Not yet." I replied, probably popping the rapper's balloon of hope. "It's barely nine A.M. The real news cycle tends to pick up at noon, four, five, six, ten and eleven. We'll know then if you're truly in the clear."

Marcus quickly got up from the chair he was seated on as his cell phone began to ring. "Shoot! It's the president of my record label."

The rapper quickly left the office, answering the phone. I let out a sigh of relief at another job well done.

"I assume the letter and picture went over well?" I heard Anthony's voice ask from the doorway.

I turned to him and nodded. "Did we have any doubts? Right now, his label will be on

top of this and make him a star again."

"And they didn't even call to thank you?"

I shook my head. "I've been doing this for five years now, trust me; this job can be thankless at times. I'm just hoping Lil Yeller stays away from any sex toy shops the next time he's

Angry."

Anthony nodded his head and I let out a sigh of relief, hoping for the best.

Chapter 2

2226 <u>**Amethyst Lane: Apartment 1B, at 6:40 P.M.**</u>
After my work days, I like to come home, kick off my boots and just take a hot shower to wash away the drama of the day. It was my way of getting the relaxation I deserved and needed.

No matter what my critics say, lying can be an exhausting job.

Ten years ago, New Fran City became what many around the world have dubbed as Hollywood 2.0. The city is plagued with various shows and movies being filmed down here thanks to the governor taking a huge grant—and tax cut—to welcome the construction of many studio lots. Thankfully, the city is big enough to house these lots and it creates new jobs and opportunities for people who weren't getting any from the original Hollywood in LA.

Hell, you can't even go to your local bodega without banging into an Oscar award winning celebrity that decided to move down here to enjoy the city's huge tax breaks.

Because of this, my job as a Hollywood Fixer becomes more important and demanding. Sure, this city has a lot more fixers or "crisis managers" as they prefer to be called, but no one is more effective at fixing a client's scandal than myself.

I dried my wet body off with a soft white cotton towel and stepped out of the shower, carefully trying my hardest not to get the white marble tiled floor wet. I wrapped the towel around my waist and let out a soft sigh as my eyes darted to the scar on my right shoulder.

The scar was made on my honeymoon night. Not because I was taking part in rough sex or anything along the lines. I fell off the canopy bed in the honeymoon suite of the Aviant Hotel—located in Scorne City—a story for another time.

I entered my bedroom and unwrapped the towel from my waist, letting the cold apartment air blow against my bare skin. I slipped into a pair of red briefs and put on a black shirt that was three times larger than my normal shirt size. It looked as if I was wearing the shirt as a dress. Something I used to do when I was younger.

My apartment gets very cold during the winter—even with the heat set on high—so having a long and loose-fitting shirt gives me some warmth to get through the nights.

I made my way into the kitchen and grabbed a glass of red wine that I'd poured myself earlier. I took a small sip and was rudely interrupted by my cell phone.

Placing the glass down on my black countertop, I grabbed my phone and saw a text message from Anthony that read: *Turn on the news now!*

I grabbed the glass of wine, walked out of the kitchen and entered the living room, grabbed the remote from the black leather sofa and turned on the television.

On the screen was a blonde news reporter standing outside of a huge prison.

The prison in question was Berger County's prison. I grabbed the remote and turned the volume up higher.

"That's right, Linda! Apparently, authorities are trying to make sense of how three prisoners were able to escape from Berger County's Prison Facility in the early hours. Two of the prisoners are Bryan Daily and his husband Maxwell Daily. They are responsible for hacking into former President Richard Powell's laptop a few years back and leaking a sex tape of him and his mistress. While they aren't a threat to society, authorities are warning about the third inmate—"

No, do not say it. Do not say his name. The last thing I need right now is to hear that name.

"None other than the leader of the Spanish Mafia, Tribu de Aries, Javi Castillo."

RRRing! RRRing! RRRing! RRRing!

The phone in my hand caused me to flinch! I looked at the caller ID to see Anthony's name and I quickly answered it. "Please tell me this is some sick joke." I stated in disbelief.

"I wish it was, Romero. I really do."

"How the hell did he even escape? Berger County Prison has maximum security!"

"If I had to take a guess, I would say it was a hell of a payout. To the right people. You and I both know how deep Javi's pockets are."

"Yeah. But still, do you think he would come down here—"

"No. He wouldn't be that stupid to come after you now. Especially when there's a huge manhunt underway. Our best option is to keep our eyes open and go about our day as if nothing happened."

Easy for Anthony to say. He and I may have known each other for only five years, but I know how men like Javi think and he is a very dangerous force that will stop at nothing to kill those who have wronged him.

As much as I want to spend hours trying to figure out where Javi would go to hide out from the police and FBI currently after him, Anthony was right. I have to keep my head on my shoulders and focus on my clients and my life here in New Fran City.

I just...I honestly just fear this night is gonna get worse.

"I know you, Romero, and I know you hate the unknown. But do not let this get to you. You have me now. I will do everything in my power to protect you."

I rolled my eyes at his words, "The last thing I need is protection. I just need to focus on my job. I'll be fine."

"I can spend the night if you'd like."

"As fun as that sounds, I'm going to pass. Seriously Anthony, I'll be fine. I just need some sleep."

"Okay. See you tomorrow bright and early."

"Yes, you will."

I hung up the phone and drank the wine in my glass. Not stopping until I swallowed every single drop.

Rrring! Rrring! Rrring!

The noise wasn't coming from the phone currently in my hand, it was coming from my other phone in the bedroom.

"Hmm, that doesn't sound good."

I got up from the sofa and walked into my bedroom. Hearing the ringing again, I got on my knees and pulled out a shoe box from under my bed.

Taking off the lid, I saw my old flip phone's screen lighting up, indicating a new text message.

I opened the phone and read through the message, unaware of the chaos that was about to unfold.

On the screen was a picture of me! In the picture I was walking through Ferrine Drive.

This photo must've been taken yesterday as I was there and wearing that same exact outfit.

I have no idea why I decided to wear a red turtleneck with a blue vest because clearly it didn't photograph well.

I scrolled down and continued reading the text.

Urgent! His name is Jayson Romero. He is a Latin male who is 5'8" tall, has brown curly hair and he is known throughout New Fran City as The Hollywood Fixer. Reward for his death is $5 Million. Reward will be submitted upon proof of his death.

I let out a silent sigh to myself.

Seconds ago, I feared things would get worse and now I've learned—spoken fears actually do come true.

<h1 style="text-align: right">Chapter 3</h1>

January 9, 2023

The front entrance of the Golden Hotel was filled with paparazzi and fans, all eager to snap a picture of the newest It couple taking over New Fran City; model Lola Han and singer Joe Lyle.

An anonymous tip on Twitter reported that the twenty- something year olds had checked into the Presidential Suite of the Golden Hotel for their first sit down interview with the Queen of Gossip, Tina Tea.

While New Fran City is proud to be Hollywood 2.0, the roadways are constantly congested, traffic is inevitable and don't get me started on the tourists that are plaguing this city like herpes during Spring Break.

But it's also a city full of celebrities who are rich and famous, and within this place are vultures that inhabit the streets watching from afar and waiting for just one slip up.

Those vultures in question would be the paparazzi. While many of the New Fran elites found them to be very problematic and immoral, they weren't breaking any laws. After all, it was their job to take the pictures and sell it to whichever magazine paid them the highest amount of money.

I parked my purple Mini Cooper a block away because I didn't want to pay a valet.

I pushed my way through the crowd approaching the hotel's golden glass doors, the door attendant opened it for me and I thanked him as I stepped foot into the lobby.

The lobby of the Golden Hotel was exactly what the namesake suggested. Furniture, light fixtures, staff uniforms, signage, napkins and even documents were all painted gold. King Midas would have been jealous.

The lobby was very spacious and it even connected with the designer Dulce Amorè's pop up shop, but I wasn't there to shop or sight see; I was there to work.

All eyes stared at me as I made my way through the packed lobby heading toward the concierge desk. I was seconds away from asking them what floor the notorious couple could be found on, when I heard someone call out my name.

I looked over toward the elevators and found Anthony standing in an open elevator holding a cup of coffee in his right hand.

"Oh, good morning beautiful!" I said, referring to the cup of coffee.

I walked over to him, grabbed the coffee from his hand and entered the elevator. He pressed button 36, causing the doors to close and the elevator to ascend.

"Meryl Hopkins left another message. She really wants you to help her."

I shook my head, opening the lid to the coffee cup. "Help her with what? Was her husband caught on Tinder again?" I replied.

Anthony shrugged his shoulders. "I honestly don't know. She wouldn't go into details with me. She just asks for you to call her back ASAP."

The aroma of the light and sweet coffee tickled my nostrils. I didn't hesitate to take a long sip, enjoying the sweet, warm and delicious taste that traveled down my throat.

Meryl Hopkins is seriously demanding my services? Either she's in it deep or she's done being triggered by gay puppets on a kid's television show.

I swallowed that sip and shrugged.

There were a few seconds of silence before Anthony started speaking again, "Did you attend that gay single mixer Sheila invited you to?"

"Anthony," I said, not wanting to hear another word about that damn single mixer our mail woman invited me to. She believed that I would find my Mr. Right at the event, but we both knew that wouldn't be the case.

"Don't you Anthony me," my assistant replied. "It's been two years since you and Salvatore divorced. I figured it would be time that you jump back in the dating game."

"As helpful as that sounds, I'm sure if I wanted to jump back in the dating game it would not be with anyone in this mess of a city. Maybe I'll date a Canadian. The French language does send tingles down my bones."

Anthony nodded. "Ah okay...that's um...good?"

"Yeah, I know." I said, taking another sip of the coffee.

"You didn't get any sleep, did you?" Anthony asked.

That was a question we both knew the answer to. Ofcourse, my lack of sleep didn't have anything to do with Javi Castillo's sudden prison break.

There was another second of silence and this one I knew was coming.

Anthony quickly pressed the emergency stop button causing the elevator to come to a screeching halt. Which in turn caused me to spill some coffee on myself. "Dammit Anthony!"

We were stuck in between the twenty-eighth and twenty- ninth floors.

"Are you seriously not going to address the elephant in the room?"

"Oh God, is my former mother-in-law in town?" I asked sarcastically.

"I got the text and I know you did too!" Anthony replied angrily. "You've been greenlit!"

I rolled my eyes, "I know that! I saw the unflattering picture and the insulting price. Five million dollars for my life? I am at least worth twenty times that."

Anthony clenched his jaws together. It's a gesture he does whenever he is annoyed.

I let out a sigh, "Look, I know this looks bad. That picture was from two days ago, which means I was being followed."

"Do you think it's—"

"No. He wouldn't waste any money on something he could do himself."

Anthony ran his fingers through his hair, completely upset. "Dammit, Romero. This is bad! You are in danger. You're going to have to leave the city."

"No!" I snapped back. "I am not going to uproot my entire life because some small dick psycho put a bounty on my head. I am better than that."

"Romero, we just survived a pandemic. People are financially desperate. A price like this will bring out anyone."

"Then let them try. I'm not some scared little boy."

I'm not scared. Things like this happen all the time. I am a fixer, I hold the secrets of the richest and most powerful people in my hands. It's not a surprise that others want me dead. I'm not going to run away because someone put a bounty on me. Running away from anything is beneath me.

"Do you at least have an idea who could've put this hit out on you?"

I arched my right eyebrow at him, "How much time do you have?"Anthony probably ran out of words to say. He knew more than anyone how stubborn I could be. Whatever plan he was trying to form in his pretty little head that revolved around me leaving New Fran City would be pointless.

"It's a good thing only hitmen got that email. If this would've hit the streets, you wouldn't be here right now."

"Gee, thanks for the faith." I retorted and Anthony pressed the button again, taking us to the next floor.

"Now," I began as I changed the subject, "what can you tell me about Hollywood's latest Romeo and Juliet story?"

"Okay, well Lola Han is twenty-two years old."

"Please tell me that isn't her real name." I chimed in.

Anthony shrugged his shoulders. "Your guess is as good as mine. She is supposedly in a relationship with pop star Joe Lyle. You know, The Homeless Singing Kid."

I looked at Anthony, clearly having no idea what the hell he was talking about, "The Homeless Singing Kid?"

"Yeah. When he was younger, someone sent a video of him singing in a cardboard box. They uploaded it to the internet and Joe was signed the next week."

That entire situation sounded like something I would concoct, props to whomever for uploading that video.

Anthony continued, "To the media, they were outed as being in a relationship last week because they were spotted together leaving a restaurant. In reality, Joe and Lola are not dating at all but Jordan Monroe has decided to create the illusion as if they were, because he manages them both."

I rolled my eyes at the mention of Jordan's name. He is the reason so many young Hollywood stars go from being rich to binging on drugs. To him, his clients are nothing more than money makers rather than actual human beings. "Where is that slimeball?"

"He called and said he's running late due to traffic. But anyway—"

The elevator took a small bump causing us both to look at the digital screen and saw we were passing the thirtieth floor.

"—Jordan hired you to prepare them for the interview with Tina Tea. You of all people know she can sniff a lie from a mile away."

Which is ironic since the 'Queen of Gossip' had no idea that for the past eighteen years, her husband was playing 'Hide the Pogo Stick' with their house cleaner.

I shook my head, calming myself down as the elevator made its way toward the thirty-fifth floor.

"This sounds like a piece of cake. I don't know why Jordan hired me. This is amateur work."

Anthony suggested, "I don't know, maybe you should take it as a compliment?"

I scoffed at his words. "A compliment from Jordan Monroe's mouth is an insult."

The elevator came to a slow stop and the doors opened. "Okay Anthony, let's go fake a Hollywood relationship."

We both walked out of the elevator to be met with a golden colored rug. I almost wanted to puke at the coloring, it was an assault on the senses. Who the hell thought this color— that looked a lot like urine—was cute to decorate the place with?

"They're in the VIP room; it's the last door on the right."

"VIP? These new Hollywood younglings sure do get treated better than the legends."

Anthony walked in front of me and led us down a long hallway, which felt like it was stretching with every step we took.

We finally reached the VIP room, which was actually the presidential suite, and Anthony knocked on the door lightly. The door opened and a young man with thinly arched eyebrows, brown short hair, pale white skin, light blue eyes and straight white pearly teeth, smiled at the sight of me. "Hello, you must be Jayson Romero. Welcome and please come in."

I took the invitation and entered the spacious and beautiful suite. The details would make the other hotel occupants jealous, but I wasn't here to bask in the beauty of the luxurious suite and quite frankly, I didn't care for the details.

"We don't have enough time to prepare before Tina and her brainless cohorts make their way up here. Should we go over anything specific?" I asked, turning around to face Joe who closed the suite's door behind Anthony.

"Not that I know of. What about you, Lola?" Joe called out.

I was born in 1993 and I remembered growing up with male pop stars who had gimmicks that differed from each other. Whether it was one who refused to wear shirts to outings or a pop star that wore assless chaps to a legend's funeral service. Yet for some reason this new generation of male pop stars looked identical to one another. They had the same thinly arched eyebrows, short brown hair that they would flip back whenever they were flirting with someone and they all wore very, very skinny jeans. Was anyone original anymore?

My concentration on the male was cut short when a young woman walked out of the bathroom with a smile on her face. "What happened, babe?"

Lola Han looked exactly like her modeling headshots. She didn't have any pores, moles, birthmarks or a blemish on her porcelain smooth face. Her baby blue eyes were round, as if she was an anime character. Her hair was duel colored. The right side was lavender and the left was a light pink.

She wore her hair up in a sleek neat bun. She also wore a floral green dress, which flowed with every move she would make.

Joe passed me by and made his way toward Lola, "This is Jayson Romero. Jordan hired him to prep us for the interview. Do you have any questions for him?"

Lola shook her head, smiling widely at the pop singer and turned her attention over to me. "Not at all. You see, when you are in love like myself, you don't need to be prepped on anything. Every and any word that comes from my mouth comes straight from my heart." She turned over to Joe and ran her fingers through his hair and he winced in disgust.

Anthony and I exchanged looks. It didn't take a genius to see how uncomfortable Joe was with Lola touching him. In addition, the fact Lola was oblivious to his state of uneasiness meant she was in denial about the plan their manager created to boost their careers.

"Anthony. Can you please take Joe out in the hall for a few minutes while I have a talk with Lola?" My tone sounded like an innocent child wanting an expensive toy from my parents. Anthony knew there was a motive behind this and he didn't bother to ask.

"Of course. Come on." Anthony opened the door and as if a fire broke, Joe ran out, leaving just Lola and I in the suite.

I waited until Anthony closed the door and I turned on the heels of my combat boots to face the oblivious love-struck girl.

"What exactly did Jordan tell you about this plan?" I asked.

The young model looked at me as if I was asking the question in a completely different language. "What plan?"

"The plan that involves you and Joe. The plan where you two pretend you have been dating for a long time to fool the public into thinking you're some kind of Hollywood royalty. Thus, getting endorsement deals, make-up lines and bookings at whatever shows cater to lonely teenage girls hoping to find their Mr. Right."

Lola shook her head at me as if I was lying. "That isn't true. You're just saying that to get me mad. I know how all you publicists work."

Apparently, a deity spent more time on her looks rather than on her brain.

"You are clearly mistaken here. Or delusional. Either way, I blame all that on the countless bleach you put in your hair." I placed the coffee cup on a nearby dresser. "You and Joe aren't really a couple. Whenever there are cameras present, you two have to get all lovey dovey for the public. But once you are both in private, you and Joe are just mere pawns in this sad, yet cliché, faux Hollywood romance concocted by a silver haired man with a midlife crisis."

The words that came out of my mouth caused Lola to clench her teeth together angrily. Her sweet girl demeanor somehow disappeared and she stormed over to me as if she was going to slap me, but she stopped a few feet away and just glared at me. "Listen to me you sad pathetic fag—"

I raised my eyebrows at her as if she had just lost her mind, but I didn't feel the need to defend myself against the entitled young model.

I just crossed my arms and listened to every word, clearly entertained by the tough facade Lola was putting on.

"I don't know what sad or twisted things are going through your mind, but Joe is my man! *My* man! He and I are not acting nor are we pretending. So, I'd advise you to stop trying to break him and I up because you have a crush on him. If you even lay one of your ugly manicured fingers on him, I will kill you and get away with it. Do you understand me?" The fire in Lola's eyes grew stronger, as did her state of insanity.

"Are you done?" I asked impatiently, bored to death with the threats.

The young model was taken aback by my reaction.

"Now understand me, sweetie. I am not interested in your 'man' because you don't have one. Joe isn't interested in you on an emotional level, just a financial one because apparently to your manager, Jordan, dating you could open many doors to his future. But if you ask me, I would've rather faked him being bisexual and dating that NFL quarterback who just came out the closet last week. Lastly, you may want to watch that tone with me, wannabe Kylie Jenner, because I will not only destroy you and watch your career burn down in flames. I will destroy you and make you relive the horror every single day of your life. Do I make myself clear?"

Throughout this speech I was calm and collected. I was angry, but I did one hell of a job not letting that anger show on my face, just in my tone. It was then that Lola probably realized I wasn't like most of the people she came across. It was also then she probably realized just how scary I could truly be.

Before Lola could respond, the suite's door opened and Anthony stood in the doorway, looking in and catching my attention. "I don't mean to interrupt but Tina is exactly five floors down."

"Great!" I said, changing my tone. "Now Joe, I need you and Lola to hold hands, but not too tightly. Whenever one of you speaks, it is imperative that the other person takes a lingering glance; it shows just how in love you two are. Also do not forget to mention that you guys have been in a relationship for six months."

Joe entered the room and lowered his perfectly arched eyebrows, "Why six months?"

I turned toward the singer and addressed him. "A week- long romance makes it obvious to the public that this relationship is nothing but a publicity stunt. In order to make the public accept this facade as real, we have to go within the six months' time frame. It makes it sound forbidden, raw, and those scavengers will get even hungrier to know why you two have chosen to keep it a secret for this long."

Joe probably understood what I meant and he was probably happy Jordan called me.

"Now any questions before the Wicked Witch of Day Time flies in?"

Joe shook his head and he glanced over at Lola, who had a look of sadness and regret on her face. She didn't bother making eye contact with me and quite frankly, I didn't care.

She just shook her head slowly, looking down at the floor.

Anthony saw Lola's reaction and glanced at me and I nodded my head at him, letting him know that everything was better now.

"Great! Now I'm not entirely sure what kind of questions she's going to ask, because I didn't receive any email from her regarding what you can and cannot answer, most likely Jordan did. I know you two will do well in improv but my main concern is with you, Lola."

Lola looked up at me, "What do you mean?"

"Tina is known for riling people up with her snarky comments and sly remarks, thus causing the celebrity she's interviewing to lose their cool and curse her out on air. Becoming a part of a bigger narrative. It's what gets her the views she needs. There is no doubt in my mind that she will try to break you and have you crack under pressure and we cannot have that."

A girl as unstable as Lola could ruin the entire plan; I secretly prayed that wouldn't be the situation here.

But she shook her head at me, "Trust me, I can handle her."

I opened my mouth to respond, but the door swung open and entering the room, was a tall bleach blonde woman. She wore a purple dress with pink polka dots, it was an eyesore for sure, but I recognized it to be the new dress from up-and-coming designer Freddo.

"I have arrived!" she sang out, giving me PTSD from when she released a heavily Autotuned song in 2000 called "In My Heart."

I let out a sigh and forced myself to give the one and only Tina Tea a smile. "Well look what crawled out fresh from her Botox party." I retorted, which caused Tina to laugh.

"Oh, aren't you a hoot Jayson ." Tina pulled in a pink leather suitcase.

"Uh, you are aware you're just here to interview them and not spending the week?"

She nodded her head at me, "Duh! I know that, silly. It's just, I'm trying this new thing now where I conduct all the interviews myself. So, I'll be in charge of microphones, direction, camera etc."

Well, this isn't going to be good.

"Oh, well good for you." I noticed how nervous both Lola and Joe were becoming. I don't blame them, the pure thought of Tina Tea directing her own interviews is scary within itself.

I flashed them a warm smile to let them know everything was going to be okay. Seriously, why do people doubt me?

I turned back to Tina who flipped her hair back and smiled, "Are you sure you're up to the task? I mean millions of people will be tuning in. This interview must go smoothly."

"I know! Which is the reason why I am so adamant about making sure this is the interview where I can make my directorial debut. With millions of people watching, I can finally be taken seriously as an Entertainment Journalist."

"And I'm all for you living your dreams. Go Tina!" I cheered for her. " But are you sure you want that kind of pressure? I can call up Flo and we still have time for her to direct this and—"

"No!" Tina spat. "I can handle this. Now, help me with these damn bags so I can set up and get this show on the road."

Anthony and Joe walked into the hall to help pull in the last two suitcases Tina had with all of her equipment inside.

Shit. Why was Tina trying something new? I'm not scared for the two love birds, but I'm more scared of whatever angle she was trying to pull.

No matter what irrational thoughts are spinning in my head, there's no point in turning back now.

Anthony and Joe entered the room holding the suitcases. "Where should we put these?"

"On the balcony." Tina replied, "I figured we would conduct the interview there and take advantage of the sunlight."

"Okay!" I clapped my hands together causing everyone to flinch. "It's show time!"

Chapter 4

Tina Tea, *mid-thirties early forties, is seated on a chair, smiling, as she gazes into the camera.*

Darlene: "Hello and good morning, New Fran City! I am your host, Tina Tea, and I am beyond thrilled to be interviewing the couple that has taken the world by storm. Joe Lyle and Lola Han."

Joe and Lola wave at the camera, smiling. They're seated. Lola is holding Joe's right hand as they look like a couple who are happily smitten with each other.

Darlene: "First off, thank you so much for coming onto my show. It is such an honor to be in the same presence as Hollywood royalty."

Joe *(smiling and shaking his head):* "I wouldn't necessarily say we are of that exact caliber. We are just two regular people. Two creative people who—he looks at Lola— were lucky enough to find each other."

Tina *(nods, still smiling):* "Let me ask the question that has everyone going crazy—wait, before I ask. Did you guys know your fans are shipping you as Dala?"

Lola and Joe shake their heads, clearly having no idea they had a relationship name.

Lola: "Not at all. That is so amazing! Our fans have been very supportive of us since...well the tabloids leaked that picture of us last week having dinner at the Grove."

Darlene: "Yes, that was my next question. Everyone wants to know how you two met since Joe is a huge pop star that sold more than twenty million records in his three-year career span and Lola...you're just...a model."

Lola smiles wide and nods her head slowly.

Joe : "That is a great question, Darlene. I was playing a show in Athens when my security received a letter from a young woman who wanted to meet me. I had no idea who this girl was. But her handwriting was beautiful. She wrote poetry that would make the strongest man cry—"

As Joe speaks, Lola stares at him lovingly.

Joe : "To make a long and boring story short, I told security I had to see who wrote me such a beautiful letter."

Tina *(in disbelief)*: "And it was Lola?"

Joe : "Not at all. It was her younger sister."

Tina lets out her signature fake laugh, sounding like a seal being strangled by a hyena.

Joe : "But as it turned out, Lola helped her write it."

Darlene: "And when was this exactly?"

Lola: "Six months ago. We've been dating for six months."

Tina *(nods in shock)*: "That is amazing! Six months in this industry is like a decade. So, make sure you two cherish each other." *She looks into the camera.* "We're going to take a quick break and when we return, Joe will tell us all about his upcoming album."

Darlene: "And cut!"

• • • •

I LET OUT A SIGH OF relief, as those two were able to pull off such an act.

Tina got up from her seat and smiled, "Great job everyone. I really thought directing this segment would be super hard, but it isn't."

I walked over to the young couple.

"How did we do?" Joe asked nervously.

"You did exceptionally well. I am so proud of both of you. Now your fans will *finally* know the truth and why you two chose to hide your love for so long."

Joe lowered his eyebrows, probably confused at my words.

Just a few minutes ago, I was telling him to act as if he could tolerate Lola and now, I started to act as if they were really a couple. He probably thought it was because Tina was in the room, but she wasn't within earshot.

"I...I don't understand-"

I pointed at my own chest, which caused both Joe and Lola to look at it in confusion. It wasn't until Lola looked at her own chest, she realized they still had the body mic on. She nudged Joe and pointed to his mic and he gave her a nod, finally understanding why my demeanor changed.

Hollywood is a tricky industry. People will smile at your face and wish you well but when you've turned your back, they're secretly on the lookout for ways to destroy you.

When it comes to microphones during interviews, it is imperative that you watch what you say; because as long as you have a hot mic on you, anything you say will be made public. Whether it was said on air or not.

A hot mic has hurt even the brightest of stars in this industry.

I smiled widely. "It seems my job here is done. I want to thank you for such an amazing job. I would hug you, but I just don't want to."

"Hey Joe." Tina interrupted, causing the young couple to look at her nervously. "I'm sorry to interrupt; I just have to say it is an honor to get to speak with you. I have been a fan of yours and I know it's awkward because of my age, but—" she placed her right hand on the young man's left shoulder and rubbed it, smiling, "I see a lot of talent in you and I know you will get far in this industry."

Lola clenched her jaws, watching the scene unfold.

I rolled my eyes and walked out of the suite, closing the door behind me, not wanting to get involved in whatever drama was about to unfold.

My job was to have them prepped for the interview and with that portion complete, as is my job here.

• • • •

A FEW SECONDS LATER:

I let out a yawn as I leaned against the wall of the elevator once the doors closed. Anthony rubbed the back of his neck, shaking his head. *"Esa Lola está loca de cojones."* (That Lola is batshit crazy.)

"That's an understatement." I snapped as the elevator started to descend. "Did Joe tell you anything about her?"

"Only the fact she has been trying to seduce him daily. He has told her many times he wasn't interested in her but she continues to make advances. Poor guy has a huge crush on his neighbor's daughter and he's stuck pretending to date a nut job that should be locked up in a psych ward."

I knew this couple was a mistake. They were completely mismatched as far as interests go.

Anthony sighed as if he had had a long day moving heavy furniture, "If you ask me Romero, I would make them break up. He deserves to just live his life doing what he wants to do. He found more success by himself. As far as I'm concerned, he doesn't need this fake romance to further his career."

Anthony was right.

"Yeah, well, this is all the work of Jordan Monroe."

The elevator slowed down and stopped in the lobby of the hotel. This shocked me, as I was sure the ride down was a lot faster than the ride up.

The doors opened and I walked out onto the lobby floor.

"Magnificent job, Romero!" A voice called out, causing every hair on the back of my neck to stand.

"Di el nombre del diablo y aparecerá." I said underneath my breath causing Anthony to chuckle.

Walking toward us was a tall older man with silver dyed hair, wearing a very tight suit. His face had not one wrinkle, which didn't shock me because while he is forty-nine years old, the man gets botox injected into his face more times than a baby burps.

"I saw the interview and I am beyond pleased with your work. Those kids were more convincing than celebrities when it comes to their charity work." Jordan waited for Anthony or I to laugh, but neither of us did, so he cleared his throat to speak.

I quickly chimed in, "When was the last time you spoke to Joe? He doesn't want to be in a relationship with her."

Jordan looked at me in shock, "He told you that?"

"He didn't have to. The poor kid just wants to tour the world and hook up with fan girls looking for something to tell their friends. He can't do that if he's dating Ms. Psychopath."

Jordan's face grew stern, well, at least that's what I thought, it was hard to tell from looking at him.

"Lola is the top selling model in Japan and I know she can hit the U.S market and be on magazine covers. She can be one of those J-Pop girls"

I rubbed my forehead in frustration at the man, who saw only dollar signs rather than anything of importance. "You would honestly have your clients be in a miserable situation just so that you could cash in on them?"

"Let me tell you something, Romero. Joe got famous because of me. I uploaded that video of him singing in a cardboard box, I dubbed him The Homeless Singing Kid. He was never homeless or even miserable with his life. He is a friend's kid that I promised to make famous. The public ate that crap up and now they will eat this up too, making Lola a star and me a billionaire."

"And you think playing bootleg Cupid is worth billions of dollars on the unhappiness of your client?"

Jordan didn't need to think about the question because it was obvious. "Don't pretend that what you do is nobler than what I do. You and I turn scraps of garbage into these beautiful and perfect illusions that the public eat up. Yes, Joe is miserable. Yes, Lola is a hot psychopath. But at the end of the day does any of that matter when they're making millions in an hour?"

Jordan combed his fingers through his silver hair and he lowered his voice so none of the hotel staff could hear the words he was saying. "Everyone sells their souls to make it in this industry and only the strong survive. Joe and Lola are both strong kids who will leave their legacy in this goddamn city and if you think—"

CRAAAASSSSSSHHHHH!!!!

Jordan's words were cut short by a loud crashing sound that came from outside of the hotel.

The horrific screams of fans camped outside caused hotel employees to run out as some of the fans ran inside, trying to take cover.

"What the hell was that?" I asked as I began to walk toward the entrance of the hotel, with Anthony and Jordan following behind.

I pushed the hotel doors open and a scene of chaos ensued. My mouth fell open as I saw what was causing the commotion and I felt as if the whole world around me slowed down.

In the middle of the street was a dead body. The only recognizable thing on the body was a pink and purple mini dress, the same mini dress Tina Tea was wearing!

"Oh my God!" I shook my head in disbelief, but the screams of a fan behind me revealed a deadlier scene.

On the curb of the hotel was a parked red sports car and on the roof of that car was the dead body of Lola Han. She was bloodied, bruised and staring lifelessly at the beautiful clear sky above her.

The chaotic scene looked like something out of a movie. Inconsolable fans, shocked, disgusted and saddened by the loss of a famous person, hotel staff scrambling and calling the ambulance and Jordan paralyzed out of shock.

I couldn't believe what I was looking at! I had just left her alive and safe upstairs seconds ago and to see her lifeless, and broken body made me sick and angry.

I stepped closer to the car without saying a word.

This could've been avoided. In fact, it should've been avoided if Jordan had decided to do the right thing and focus on Joe 's career instead of forcing him into a relationship he clearly didn't want.

Nevertheless, it was too late now.

Too late to blame anyone.

Too late to think of possible outcomes and most importantly; too late to feel guilty.

I slowly looked up at the balcony of the thirty-sixth floor, swearing I could see a figure staring down at the tragic scene below with a smile of relief on his face.

Joe always sang about paradise in his songs and how he just wanted to smile under the sun. Based on the chaos down on the streets, I'm sure he found his paradise and finally the freedom he had longed for.

Chapter 5

January 16, 2023:

After the past week, I've felt the need for coffee increase rapidly. Joe was cleared of all charges as surveillance videos showed Lola push Tina off the balcony. Apparently, Lola lost her footing and it wasn't long until she too fell over.

Once that graphic video hit the airwaves—thanks to Anthony's impeccable hacking skills—Joe was no longer a suspect and he fired Jordan.

I just want today to go by smoothly, without any surprises.

I tapped my boot on the floor of the elevator as it took me up to the third floor of 3269 Merlaut Rowe, which is where my agency, *Fame Fixer Inc, has* been based for the past five years.

I was able to purchase this building after the death of my abuela, who left me a hell of an inheritance. I had no idea what I wanted to do with it at the time.

I knew that I wanted to be a fixer for celebrities after I got my public relations degree, but the only job that came close to public relations was interning for the city's top crisis manager, Lois Grant.

I took the job and I was great at what I did, I learned so much from Lois.

Sadly, she died in 2018 and her moronic son shut down her business and laid everyone off. It was difficult for me to find a job after that, which is why I decided to create *Fame Fixer Inc.*

The elevator finally stopped on the third floor, the doors opened and I walked toward the frosted glass door *Fame Fixer Inc.*

I pushed open the glass door to hear Anthony laughing, a sound that was rare, seeing how he wasn't one to laugh hysterically as if he had just heard a joke. I looked to find Anthony standing by his desk and speaking to an olive-skinned man. A man I'd never thought I would see again. The man was 5'11" tall, had short black hair that was slicked back with gel, a chiseled face, and a muscular body frame, which was revealed through his tight, buttoned up purple and red shirt and gray designer pants. They stopped talking and turned to me.

"Hey, Romero, this is—"

"Oliver Morales. Top private investigator of Torne City," I replied.

Oliver smiled proudly at me as if I was a celebrity who just retweeted him. "So, you've heard of me?"

I nodded. "Yes, I have, but don't let it go to your head, I've heard of you only because you're a dick and I always have to know my dicks just in case I need one."

Okay, so I must admit that sounded like a euphemism, but since Oliver is a private investigator, he is considered a Dick. Why? Well, during the nineteenth century, a private investigator was someone who watched his or her mark, apparently the word *dick* was defined as 'to watch'. Fascinating, isn't it?

"Well, that's quite interesting," Oliver began. "Because I've heard a lot about you."

"Not many nice things, I'm sure," I replied, causing Oliver to shrug his shoulders.

"I'm not one for gossip. But someone did say you had a hump and eight legs. Clearly that was false information."

I let out a chuckle. "How do you know? Maybe I have the hump hidden away somewhere and my extra legs only come out when I'm about to attack my prey."

Oliver let out a laugh that was deep and authentic. Living in New Fran City for this long, it's easier to spot the fake laughs from the ones that are real.

"Well, it's an honor to be in your presence, Jayson Romero. Although I'm not sure if I should be honored or scared."

I gave him a sly smirk. "Go with both. It's more fun that way. Now, may I ask what you're doing in my office?"

He cleared his throat and said, "There has been a recent string of car thefts within the block. The person who hired me to investigate, believes that it's the work of an underground car theft ring. Where they steal cars for parts and sell them on the black market."

Really? That's what he's going with?

Merlaut Rowe is home to rich White guys who hire people to run their businesses and then the owners take their private jets to whatever private island they recently purchased. They never return to their businesses unless it's for tax season or the holidays. They didn't care about the wellbeing of their employees or let alone cars.

He still didn't answer my question. "And you're here in my office because?"

"Well, one of two reasons." Oliver stated, "The first reason was to see if your car has been stolen."

"It hasn't." I quickly interjected. "I always park it on the curb in front. No one ever touches it."

He nodded again slowly, probably taking mental notes in his head on my body language, tone etc.

"What kind of car do you have?"

"A purple Mini Cooper."

Oliver nodded, smiling, and I could see Anthony glaring at him. "And secondly, your cameras outside point across the street to where my client had their car broken into. I was wondering if I can take a look at the footage from three days ago and—"

"Absolutely not." I found myself interjecting again.

Oliver didn't budge with my answer. "May I ask why?"

"I didn't think I would have to point it out to you, but here I go." I inhaled deeply and began to tell him the exact reasons why he would not be looking at the footage recorded. "My clientele list ranges from A-list celebs to politicians. They come to me because they can trust me to keep their secrets. It's a no-brainer that seeing them leave my door, or let alone seeing them enter this building, would cause the blogs to run with insinuations."

"I understand your concern, Mr. Romero"

"Jayson," I corrected him.

Once again, Oliver nodded. "I understand your concern, but my only reason for being here is to get a lead on what happened to my client's car. I was told you own this building and I know the cameras were running that night. I have no interest in whomever enters this building. Just on what happened to the car. Trust me, that's all I want."

"I'll counter that offer." I retorted, "And instead Anthony can get access to the footage, look through it and show you only what happened to your client's car. Deal?"

Oliver didn't have much of an option here. He flashed me a smile that revealed his dimples and he slowly licked his lips.

Oh God, was he seriously trying to flirt with me to change my mind?

It was clear as day that he wanted to see the footage but I wasn't going to let that happen.

"That's a great idea." Anthony interrupted, "I can look through it now."

Oliver rolled his eyes at me and then turned to Anthony, "Great. Let's get this ball rolling."

"Great." I said, "I'll just be in my office making phone calls and hoping none of my clients got caught in a college submission scandal."

I turned around and began to walk a few feet away into my private office, where I closed the door trying my hardest not to make it obvious that I hated the idea of Oliver in my office.

Before I could at least unbutton my jacket to settle in and start my morning, my office phone began to ring.

I walked toward the phone and quickly answered, "Romero."

"Good morning, Jayson. This is Meryl Hopkins calling."

I didn't need an introduction from her. Her voice has always been so prestigious, throughout her fifty year long career span in this industry. Her voice was soft and her English accent made her sound as if she was royalty—of course her vanity did that for her as well.

"Good morning, Meryl," I replied, not really wanting to stroke her ego as it was still early in the morning and I have a noisy PI just outside of my office door. "Let me guess, you're calling because you've changed your mind about wanting to leak that story about your husband cheating on you to the press?"

"Oh, my goodness!" she gasped, causing me to roll my eyes, "How did you know?"

"Because this is the tenth time this week you've changed your mind."

"It is a very big deal, Jayson . What you're suggesting is that I use private and incriminating evidence of my husband's infidelity to destroy his image and his career."

"No." I replied. "Infidelity won't destroy his career, unless he's a YouTuber or something. What it does is undermine whatever secret he is threatening to tell the public about you."

It was a very amazing and elaborate plan! One that I've done plenty of times before.

He is threatening Meryl by saying he's going to go public with intimate secrets about her. If I get the videos and photos of him cheating on her out to the public, before he makes any revelations; the public will see him as being vindictive and a liar. Thus disregarding anything he's spewing as facts, but painting him as a man trying to save his own ass.

But alas, she has decided to change her mind, which once again ruins that plan.

"I understand, but he and I are working things out."

"Again?" I didn't realize this question came out of my mouth until I heard it.

"Yes. I'm sure you are dating someone or have dated someone and you've gone through your ups and downs."

I have. And I did. But it clearly wasn't this bad.

"Look Meryl, I just want to make sure that you are okay."

"And I am. To prove it to you, why don't you come over for dinner?"

"As tempting as that sounds—" It didn't. "I have a few clients I have to meet with today. So, I'll

definitely take a rain check."

"Great! Thank you so much for everything. Hey, did I ever tell you the story about the time my panties were showing on the red carpet?"

"No, and please don't."

Meryl Hopkins may be Hollywood royalty but she does have a problem with oversharing at times.

I wished her well and hung up the phone, letting out a sigh of frustration. Yet before I could even hear myself think, the office phone began to ring again.

This time I answered it quickly. "Look, I do not want to hear about your panties showing on the red carpet!" I stated on the phone.

"I'm not sure what you've heard, Boots. But I always go commando on red carpets." a familiar voice said on the phone causing chills to run down my spine.

That masculine voice, which was smooth like velvet and smothered in a Cuban accent belonged to Salvatore Maldonado—my ex-husband.

"What do you want?" I asked, cutting straight to the point.

"Estás desnudo en mi escritorio cubierto de crema batida y bañado en jarabe de chocolate." *(You naked on my desk covered in whip cream and smothered in chocolate syrup.)*

I rolled my eyes. "Ah, ya veo. Bueno, perdiste ese privilegio una vez que el juez firmó los papeles del divorcio." *(You kinda lost that privilege when the judge finalized our divorce.)*

He chuckled on the other line, "Is it safe to talk?"

"It is. Depending on what you want to talk about of course."

"I just wanted to see how you were doing. I know you get very...what's the word? Caótico, this time of year."

"Chaotic? Me? Chaotic?" I let out a loud "Ha!" which caused him to chuckle in my ear. "I'm fine. I've been keeping busy and I've been going out on dates with guys, so yeah. I'm far from chaotic."

Why the hell did I lie to him and tell him that I was going on dates, as if I wanted to make him jealous? I shook my head, wanting to go back in time or just shove my foot in my mouth.

"You've been going on dates?" He asked as if he knew I was lying.

"Yep. I mean, we're divorced, so I'm granted that right."

Silence fell between us. "Eres un gran mentiroso. Especialmente para aquellos que no te conocen. ¿Pero yo? Vamos, Boots, ahora solo me estás insultando." *(You are a great liar. Especially to those who don't know you. But me? Come on Boots, now you're just insulting me.)*

I hated how well he knew me. "Why are you calling me?" I asked, making it obvious I had no rebuttal to his claims.

"How about we have dinner next week?"

"You and I have dinner? Not sure if that's a good thing or bad."

There were a few seconds of silence on Salvatore's end before he answered, "Why would it be a bad thing? We're two grown men having dinner."

"Two grown men who used to be married to one another." I corrected him.

"Look, Boots, we divorced on good terms. We don't have any hostility toward each other and not to mention with your birthday coming up, I think it would be a great way to celebrate it...to do things right this time."

Was that an apology? Knowing Salvatore for as long as I have, he wasn't one to apologize to me, or to anyone.

For three of the six years I've known him, he always forgot my birthday. He would blame it on his own plans or on his job, but this year he's owning up to his one flaw he had in our relationship. That's a huge step for Salvatore Maldonado.

"Hmm, alright fine. You can take me out for my birthday. Next Thursday, I'll be free at eight."

"Alright. I can—"

"Wait! Is this going to be one of those cliché dinners where you tell me you're about to get married to someone else and you're looking for my blessing?"

"What? No." Salvatore replied, causing me to let out a sigh of relief.

The last thing I needed was to deal with *that*.

"I assure you—" he chuckled, "I am single and there's no wedding and no secret family. I just want to see you."

I found myself smiling again and I cleared my throat, not wanting to let him hear that I was happy with his words.

"Okay good. Not that I was worried about it or anything."

"Nice try, Boots. And thank you for answering the phone. It was great to hear your voice again."

"I know." I replied and he said his goodbye, I said mine and hung up the phone.

I met Salvatore Maldonado six years ago when I was at some pretentious Hollywood executive party in Starlight Hills. The party wasn't my cup of tea. At the time I was working for Lois Grant and she wanted me to scope out potential clients. Her idea of scoping out potential clients involved talking to strangers and asking them about their private lives. I took a different approach.

I had my camera phone on me and decided to record every celebrity taking part in something stupid during the party, like: cheating on their spouses, doing drugs, talking bad about their bosses and fans. Once I got the videos I needed, I would then meet them the next day and show them everything they said on camera. It was a perfect set up; unfortunately, Lois didn't see it that way. Then again, she never really agreed with my methods.

As I stood by the sideline and recorded married actor Mark Romes sucking face with a female server, Salvatore stood beside me, sipping a bottle of beer he had snuck in.

"You know, I'm not one to judge, but I'm pretty sure the world wide web contains numerous videos that you could watch to get your rocks off," he said, which caused me to quickly put my camera phone away.

I turned to look at him and I was in awe at what I saw.

Not only did the six-foot tall, twenty-eight-year-old Cuban man with soft black hair, mocha-colored skin and dimples when he smiled, caught my attention. But it was the fact he was daring, honest (probably too honest at times) and he had a dark sense of humor that would make the Addams family blush.

I couldn't believe that I never met a man as real as him here in New Fran City, and then he told me what he does for a living, and I knew why I never met a man like him before; he works for the government as an expert in professional pseudocide!

Pseudocide is when someone would fake their own death. So, the fact the government has a division with experts who help politicians, celebrities, athletes, etc., fake their deaths, is a troubling thought.

I never cared to ask him who his clients were because I, more than anyone, understood the privacy of our clients. We always found a way to separate business from pleasure, except on two occasions which had him and I working to help a rock star and a senator.

It wasn't until our tenth date that we made love for the first time. He was gentle, mindful, caring and yet dominant when the time arose. We spent every weekend together, because our careers kept us busy and it wasn't a problem for us.

We got married on March 30th, 2018.

He served me with divorce papers on January 20, 2021. The marriage didn't end because of cheating but it ended when he just said out of nowhere he wanted a divorce. As much as I tried to get an explanation on why he felt like this, he moved off the grid.

The finalization of the divorce process was easy, considering we both signed pre-nups and agreed that we didn't want any property or money from the other.

I had gotten letters from him for my birthday, anniversary, and other holidays that we would celebrate together, I burned them and never cared to read any of them.

Why would I? He broke my heart by leaving me, something he promised me he would never do!

I fell in love with him because he accepted every part of me, the crazy, the good, the bad. Unfortunately, he never gave me a chance to tell him the truth about my past.

.

.

.

A past that I fear will haunt me sooner than I had originally thought.

Do I still love him? Of course, I do. And I know he loves me, too. Just because we got divorced, it doesn't mean we hate each other, just the timing was off for us both.

Knock! Knock!

"Come in," I said, finally taking off my jacket.

The door opened and I was expecting to see Anthony or Oliver standing in the doorway, but instead it was Jordan Monroe!

Great! This day just keeps getting better.

Chapter 6

I looked behind him to see Anthony clenching his jaws and heading straight for the door.

"I hope you don't mind, San Juan, I just waltzed right in." Jordan stated.

"It's Jayson." I corrected him, although he knew my name he just said these racist things to get under my skin.

I looked at his tight designer suit and shook my head, smirking, "And must I say, you look mighty dapper for someone who's number one client fired him for fleeing the country after his traumatic incident."

"Oh, that's what you think happened? Oh no. I just decided to visit my aunt in Canada, she's very sick and ummmm—"

I ignored Jordan's stammering and gave Anthony a nod, indicating that I would be fine.

There was clearly something on Jordan's mind, so I wanted to hear him out.

"And it's fine. Just in the future, try to call before you pass by. My assistant enjoys shooting trespassers."

"Oh? Pablo is packing?" he chuckled.

"Lucky for you, he isn't today." I sat down on my chair, "Please come in. Let's not drag this out any longer than it has to be."

Jordan closed the door and sat down on the chair in front of my desk.

Jordan Monroe is the type of Caucasian man you would find soliciting night clubs, trying to pick up women decades younger than him. He wore tight designer suits that showed no muscles, but in his head he was probably built like Henry Cavill.

I expected Jordan to tell me how his life is falling apart after Joe fired him and hired *me* to be his new publicist, but instead he leaned in and said, "I want in."

Those three words caused me to lower my eyebrows and I repeated them in my brain. "What are you talking about?"

"Whatever this operation is. I want in."

I shook my head, still not understanding where Jordan was going with his words.

"Oh, don't play dumb, Jayson. There are three other PR Crisis Firms in New Fran City. Each of them are staffed with about seventy people. This is the only agency where it's just you and your assistant. Yet you get all the hot clients. How is that possible?"

"Need I remind you I worked in the shadows of the amazing and late Lois Grant, God rest her soul. She taught me everything I needed to know about public relations."

"Bullshit!" Jordan stated, completely disregarding the lie I told. "Lois died broke and alone. She lost all her clients, when that Ken doll she called a son, let her staff go. A bunch of them had to move back to New York City because there were no jobs here. Then you swooped in and created your own agency. It's suspicious."

I shrugged my shoulders, smiling, "I'm just great at what I do. I mean after all, you thought so too when you hired me to help your clients fake their relationship."

"Because you're affordable and come with an impeccable reputation." He unbuttoned his light blue blazer and leaned back in the chair; making it clear he had a lot more to say.

"Which has me believing this operation is a gimmick."

I had to refrain from laughing, "A gimmick?"

"Yeah. The rent in this town is at least three thousand dollars a month, the renovations here probably cost $500,000. What the hell are you doing in the shadows to stay afloat and how can I be a part of it?"

I have to give the man his props, he knew his basic math. "Look, Jordan, I'm sure you have many theories spinning inside of that obviously sprayed tanned head of yours, but I assure you, *Fame Fixer Inc* is a legit agency. I choose not to expand my staff because I don't need to. I have connections with various people because my past clients have recommended me, but in no way is what I do here illegal."

Jordan nodded slowly, not even blinking once, he was clearly studying my facial expressions and my body language to see if I was lying.

"Okay, then how are you twenty-nine years old and own an agency that's worth millions?"

"I have to say it's due to my colorful personality." I gave him a wink and pretended that I received a text on my cell phone because this conversation is lasting longer than it should be. "I have to call this client back, but thank you for showing up here. Again, I am so sorry one of your clients is dead and the other fired you."

Jordan rose up from the seat slowly, "Fine, don't tell me. But I will find out what you're hiding and you're going to wish you took me up on my offer."

With that Jordan turned around, opened the door and walked out of my office.

My smile faded once Anthony stood in the doorway and he asked, "Everything good here?"

I shook my head, watching as Jordan left *Fame Fixer Inc*, "Guess we're going to have to wait and see."

Chapter 7

January 17, 2023, at York City, 6:35 P.M.

I hate weddings! Not sure why, I've just always had.

My own wedding took place in the New Fran Courthouse, because neither Salvatore or I had family to invite so we didn't want to make it a great big spectacle.

However, I decided to put on a brave face for the wedding of Ryan Lake and Alice Parr.

Ryan was a former client of mine who hired me to help him land the lead role in the movie adaptation of the hit erotic book series, *Shades of Caine*. He wanted more than anything to play the lead role of Gregory Caine, a sex addicted billionaire. But that role was being sought out by many of Hollywood's elite, and seeing how Ryan was an eighties heartthrob famous for playing the boy next door in the hit series *Cluemore*; it was not a shocker when the suits at the studio refused to let him audition.

But I had a plan, I always have a plan.

I decided to hire adult film actress Alice Parr to be Ryan's scene partner. They were going to recreate a scene in the book where Gregory ties up a bartender and uses her as his own personal sex toy. The scene was hot, but Alice and Ryan's chemistry was even hotter.

Sadly, the audition tape was leaked and the studio refused to cast him, but Ryan and Alice ended up signing a huge deal to an adult film company, making them exclusive partners.

I guess somewhere along the line they fell in love and decided to—stupidly—get married.

Hence why I'm twenty minutes out of New Fran City at a church wearing a very tight blue and black suit that I am going to burn once I get home.

The wedding ceremony only lasted twenty minutes and then we had to drive a block away to a beautiful castle where the reception was being held.

The castle would make Cinderella and Prince Charming jealous! It was so huge that I wanted to get lost just exploring it. The reception was in a courtyard, which had a pond and rose bushes in the shape of hearts. It honestly looked like something the Queen of Hearts would have in Wonderland.

I made my way over to the free bar and sat down at the counter. "What will you have?" the bartender asked with a wide smile on his face.

Something stiff! Was the answer I said in my head, but I'm driving back home when this is all over so I couldn't get as drunk as I wanted to.

I exhaled and replied, "Just a Coke."

The bartender nodded and took out an ice-cold bottle of Coke from the cooler.

"Huh, I pegged you for a Pepsi guy." I heard a very familiar voice causing me to turn around to see the ugliest sight there, Jordan Monroe.

I rolled my eyes at him, "Good God, what the hell are you doing here? Found another client that you're going to manipulate, causing them to snap?" I asked as I took the soda the bartender gave me and took a small sip, letting the bubbles tickle the back of my throat.

I didn't bother to look at whatever ensemble Jordan decided to wear because everything he decides to wear looks horrible and ill fitting.

"No. I'm a friend of the bride. Well, really her number one client when she used to work as a prostitute."

Ugh! Could this man be any more offensive?

"So..." he leaned in toward me and lowered his voice, "Have you given any thought to my proposal for wanting into your business?"

Here comes this midlife crisis once again, insinuating that my agency is something more than me helping clients. Seriously, this man was starting to get on my last nerve.

I placed the glass on the counter and turned to Jordan, giving him one of my infamous smiles, "Listen to me you walking-sad-excuse-of-a-man. I told you once that I have no idea what weird scenario you cooked up in your pea sized brain but you and I will never work together. Do I make myself clear?"

I kept my tone to a calming yet sinister one as I didn't want the group of people who were dancing to think I was insulting the man, I mean I was, but still. I had to do it with grace and poise.

Jordan returned the smile, "You might want to watch your tongue with me, boy. I will take you down quicker than the iceberg took down the Titanic."

Oooh, a challenge? And here I thought this day was going to be dull and boring.

"Oh, sweet, sweet Jordan. Pooky pie, I will destroy you and what'll be left is that toupee on your head and the balls your ex-wife still possesses."

I expected Jordan to have a snappy comeback, but he instead grabbed my arm and tightly gripped it causing me to glare at him. "You need to watch that mouth before I put it to good use."

I opened my mouth to retort, but then I heard a voice approach and ask "Is everything okay here?"

I looked over to find Salvatore Maldonado, aka my ex- husband, standing there.

I lowered my eyebrows, not expecting to see him at the wedding dressed in a black suit and tie that didn't do much to hide the fact he lost weight and...gained muscles?

"Oh, everything is fine, Dick." Jordan muttered, releasing my arm and still flashing his veneer filled smile at me. "I was just reminding Jayson over here, how much I enjoy his job in New Fran City."

I nodded my head, "And I was just reminding Jordan that I carry and have an amazing trigger finger and impeccable aim."

With that the man got up and walked away, getting lost in the sight of a nearby bridesmaid who was clearly drinking more than she should've been.

Salvatore let out a sigh and sat down next to me at the bar, "I see you're still making friends."

I rolled my eyes at his words, smiling, and shrugged. "You know me, I'm always sociable." I took a sip of the soda, swallowed, and looked at my ex, "What exactly are you doing here? You told me you were coming into town next week."

"Yeah, to meet up with you. I had no idea you were invited to this wedding."

"I know the couple."

"And I know the bride." He replied, clearing his throat, which was a huge indication that he knew her professionally, which meant Alice Parr is not even her real name.

Seeing Salvatore again made me want to hug him tightly and never let him go! But we're at a wedding reception full of people who are famous around Hollywood and the last thing I need are the blogs picking up the fact I was hugging my ex- husband at a wedding...well the fun part about it, is that I'm so amazing at my job with manipulating the public and hiding secrets, that no one but my close friends—okay just Anthony—knew that Salvatore and I were married!

So, it was just a matter of me not wanting to be on the five o'clock news hugging a mystery man.

Salvatore cleared his throat again. Although he was smiling at me—giving me that same smile from our first date—I knew there was something on his mind.

"What is it?" I asked calmly, yet tried my best to hide how nervous I was.

The Cuban man, who always dressed sharp and had mannerisms that reminded me of Manny Ribera from Scarface, looked around the crowd of people and he returned to look at me, "Let's take a walk. We have a lot to talk about."

Well, that doesn't sound too good.

• • • •

THE DJ BEGAN TO PLAY some annoying music I assumed was a one hit wonder from the nineties.

Salvatore and I decided to walk around the huge castle property. It faced a river, some benches and it was the only area that didn't serve alcoholic beverages, so it was the perfect place for us to be alone in.

As we walked side by side, I couldn't help but smile, remembering the nights after dinner where we would walk through the local park talking about our days while holding hands.

I guess Salvatore must've seen me smile, because he asked, "What is it?" with a smile as well.

I shook my head, "Just bringing back a lot of memories of us walking through the park."

"Ah *si*, I remember. It was honestly the highlight of our days. Just to be outside in nature, holding you and not worrying about the craziness we endure at work."

We approached a bench that was very far from the wedding reception, and he motioned for me to sit. I did and then I looked at him, "What is going on?" I asked again, hoping this time he would answer the damn question.

Salvatore sat beside me and he inhaled and then let out a deep exhale that sounded more like a sigh of regret. "As you remember, in order to fully do my job, I go undercover as an assassin to look for bounties. Then I intercept the bounty hunters from their targets by finding them, faking their deaths, making it look real and then taking the credit."

Yes, I remember all of that. Which is why he always wore a blond wig, blue contacts and went by the name Dylan Bregar. I knew all of this already, but I guess after two years of being divorced he needed to brag about it to someone.

I nodded slowly, kind of knowing where he was going with this but hoping he wasn't heading in that direction.

He looked at me and I met his eyes, "Boots...someone put a hit out on you."

I guess this is the part where I should've gasped and clenched my chest in disbelief and shock. Or at least, that's probably what he wanted me to do since he told me this as if I had no idea.

"I know it's probably a lot to take in, but please, just know I am here and I have a plan."

I nodded and squinted at him, wondering how long it would take for him to realize this was no news to me.

He nodded, finally getting the hint. "And you already know about the hit."

I once again nodded and he rose up to his feet. "*¡Maldita sea! Aquí estaba preocupado por ti y preguntándome cómo ibas a tomar la noticia solo para que me dijeras que ya sabías sobre la recompensa. ¡Te juro que si aún estuviéramos casados me llevarías a una tumba prematura por preocuparme por ti!*"

I smiled as Salvatore continued with his Cuban tirade. Once he calmed down, I began to speak, "Hey don't get mad at me!" I retorted, "I have connections, did you forget?"

"I did!" he rubbed his forehead and placed a hand on his hip. "I was trying to find ways to protect you."

"Protect me?" I chuckled. "So, your idea of protection was to wait until next week to tell me that someone wants me dead?"

"No, I was following up on a few leads to see who put the hit out on you."

"And did you find any?"

He shook his head and once again started on a Cuban tirade of words that not even I knew.

I quickly rose to my feet and grabbed Salvatore's hands and looked into his eyes, smiling. "Take a breather there, Tiger. I am eternally grateful that you are worried about me. And I'm so happy I didn't key your car the day you served me divorce papers. Because then you wouldn't care like you do."

Whenever Salvatore would go through a tough day at his job, I would grab his hands and stare into his eyes. We always joked that I was the Beauty to his Beast. Although that story is more about Stockholm Syndrome than as romantic as I'm trying to make it sound..but my point was made.

"I'm fine. Everything is going to be fine. Anthony told me this email hit more of the assassin's hotlines than any local gangs. You and I both know the organized assassins are very quiet and calculating about their moves. If they wanted me dead, they would have done so already. But best believe, I am fine."

I'm sure Salvatore wanted to spend the next few minutes arguing about whether I was truly fine or not, but I wasn't really in the mood.

"Now, how about we head back to the party and see if there are any Hot Pockets left over." While I was about to walk back toward the party hoping Salvatore would follow me, he grabbed my arm and pulled me closer to him.

Before I knew it, he kissed my lips softly and held me tightly. His tongue entered my mouth and I found myself softly sucking on it.

Minutes passed by before I pulled away and looked around, hoping no one caught that. "What was that for?" I asked calmly, clearly not complaining but very curious as to why he decided to kiss me.

"I don't know. I mean...was it bad? Should I not have done that? I don't know the etiquette of what ex-husbands should do when they see each other again."

There he goes again, overthinking everything. Although I couldn't help but wonder the same thing.

I didn't care if us kissing was wrong because I haven't been with anyone in the past two years and I missed having a man grab me tightly and kiss me. But was this proper for us?

I smiled and shook my head, "No, I loved it. It was good and screw what the etiquettes are."

"Yeah, screw it." he replied.

Before I could say anything or let alone think it, my phone started to vibrate in my pocket. I apologized as I took it out. "It's Anthony." I said, reading the caller ID.

"He still works for you?" Salvatore asked, letting out a sigh.

It was obvious that he never liked Anthony, and my assistant felt the same way about him.

When I asked Salvatore about his weird dislike of Anthony, he told me "It's obvious." but never once dwelled much on the subject. Whatever Salvatore assumed was going on between Anthony and I was completely wrong—trust me!

"You should answer it." Salvatore said, "Might be something important."

"Or just him calling to ask if I'm coming back before the New Fran Hunters play against the Torne City Jetters game, he got tickets for."

If any of my clients needed me, they would get in direct contact with me, instead of the office. That's why they all have my cell phone number.

"Now." I smiled, wrapping my arms around the back of Salvatore's neck, "Where were we?"

"Hmm, I think we were doing this." He leaned down and we started to make out again.

I closed my eyes and moaned into his mouth as his hands slid down my back and grabbed my rear end tightly.

I was always submissive to him in the bedroom. Sure, I'm dominant in my career and I always command the room anywhere I go, but when I was with Sal, I would let him take the reins in the bedroom. We meshed well because I knew my place as a proud bottom and he knew I would worship him as the top.

But those rules only applied to the bedroom.

Bzz! Bzz! Bzz! Bzz! Bzz!

Shit!

I pulled away from the kiss and once again took the phone out to see Anthony's name on my caller ID.

It wasn't like him to call me twice, once was good enough.

Something is clearly wrong.

"I'm sorry, I have to take this."

Salvatore nodded, agreeing with me, and I quickly answered the phone, "What's wrong Anthony?"

"Romero, I need you to come back to the office. Meryl's here, looking for you."

"Are you serious? Can't you tell her I'm busy with another client, because I am really not in the mood for her crap."

Anthony's voice cracked. "I did and she said she isn't leaving. Romero, just get back here ASAP. This is an emergency!"

"I'm in York City. I'll be there as fast as I can. Hold her off." I hung up and let out a sigh in frustration.

"Is everything okay?" Salvatore asked in concern.

"One of my former clients is at the office and won't leave. Anthony claims it's an emergency. I gotta go."

"I can drive you. I know a few shortcuts that will have you back in five minutes."

I opened my mouth to say something, but as if Salvatore was a telepath he retorted with "I'm not asking, I'm telling you. Get in my car now!"

"Ugh fine! So bossy." I playfully replied, walking toward the reception as Salvatore followed, unsure of what the hell awaited me back at my office.

• • • •

THE OFFICE OF *Fame Fixer Inc*:

The elevator stopped on the third floor of my office building.

I quickly walked out of the elevator to find Anthony standing by the doorway leading into the spacious office.

"Where is she?"

Anthony looked at me. "Inside your office, but you should know…" I ignored his words and stormed inside, passing by the beautifully decorated waiting area, which was painted pink and black.

The waiting area was filled with a few pink and black leather recliners, a large plasma television screen, a table, which always had the best food catered from the Italian restaurant down the street and a pink and black decorated Christmas tree, that neither Anthony nor I had the energy to take down.

I pushed open my office door to find the fifty-eight-year- old actress standing by my desk watching an old movie she starred in years ago, which was playing on the television screen.

"Oh, dahling! Can you believe I was about your age when I did this film?" She asked, not taking her eyes off the black and white movie currently playing.

I placed my hands on my hips. "You cannot barge into my office without an appointment. I don't care who you are!"

Meryl Hopkins paid me no mind and she kept her eyes glued to the screen. I only saw the back of Meryl, and for some odd reason she was wearing a pink silk robe.

"Are you listening to me?" The actress still didn't flinch, and I clenched my jaws.

After what unfolded in the past six minutes, the last thing I needed was an incoherent Hollywood actress thinking she was better than anyone and everyone because she had a few Oscars on her trophy shelf.

"Meryl!" I finally shouted, causing the woman to break out of her hypnotic stare. She slowly turned around to face me, and I couldn't believe what I was looking at.

On the front of Meryl's robe was a large stain of fresh blood and her eyes were red, as if she was crying. "Meryl, are you okay?"

She gave me a smile and calmly replied, "Oh yes, dahling. The blood isn't mine. It's my husband's."

The statement made me worry even more. "What did you do?"

"I hit him over the head with my Oscar." She paused and met my gaze. "Oh, by the way! Did you hear, dahling? I'm going to be honored with a Lifetime Achievement award at the Oscars. Isn't that grand?" The woman's tone changed from traumatic to calm and pride within a matter of seconds.

All I could do at this point was run my fingers through my hair in frustration.

Chapter 8

J**anuary 20, 2021, at 8:20 P.M.**

I pushed the door open to my apartment and held my boots in my hands. I threw them in a plastic bin and took off my face mask, finally able to breathe in the cinnamon aroma of my apartment.

"Honey, I'm home!" I called out as I started to strip down to my underwear, placing each article of clothing into a plastic bag.

The pandemic has caused many people in the city of New Fran to alternate their daily routines. On my normal day after work, I would come home, open a bottle of wine and just uncoil as I cook dinner. If Salvatore was home, he would probably bend me over the counter and make love there in the kitchen as the food bakes in the oven. But that was no longer the option for us.

Salvatore had lost a few friends and colleagues from this strain of the COVID variant and the last thing any of us wanted was to get infected as well.

Which explains why I'm walking over to the bathroom right now in my underwear.

I entered the tub, pulled my underwear down, threw it in another plastic bin and started the water, waiting until it was a decent temperature before I turned on the shower.

"Hey. I didn't hear you come in." I heard Salvatore say as he entered the bathroom.

"Let me guess, you were playing that game Fortday again?"

He let out a chuckle, "That's not what it's called and I think you know that." I heard him unzip something and I smirked, realizing he's probably going to join me in the shower.

"How was your day?" I asked, taking the soap bar and lathering myself, smelling the lavender scent that emitted from the bar.

"It was okay. Nothing too eventful. How about yours?"

The shower curtain opened and I turned to see my husband standing before me, completely naked and aroused. His mocha-colored skin was starting to get wet from the hot running water raining down from the shower head. I placed my soap bar back in its dish and grabbed a different bar of soap which I used to rub all over Salvatore's hairy chest.

"Spent my day fixing the reputation of an actress who decided to cry and call the organizers of the Sand Desert Palooza 'selfish and ignorant' for canceling the event due to COVID. So, there was that."

He laughed and shook his head. "*Le persone sono davvero stupide, vero?*" (People are really stupid, aren't they?)

I nodded and started to rub my hands down toward his length, which began to harden even more from my touch.

I slowly jerked it off as he licked his lips, moaning. "Boots..."

"Yeah?" I asked as I tiptoed to kiss the right side of his neck.

"Boots...I...mmmmm...I want a divorce."

I pulled away and stepped back, looking at him in anger, "What?!"

• • • •

"ROMERO?" THE SOUND of Anthony's voice caused me to snap out of the flashback I was having of that horrible night.

I got up from the sofa and walked over to the hallway where Anthony was descending the stairs, holding the corpse of Meryl's husband wrapped in plastic over his right shoulder. On his hands, he wore black leather gloves and plastic bags covered both his shoes.

"Is everything cleaned up?" I asked, not even batting an eye.

He nodded as he got off the last step. "His DNA is gone, as well as hers. The Oscar is bleached. Her bedroom is the cleanest room in this house."

"Perfect. Where are you dumping him?" I asked, watching as Anthony began to walk toward the kitchen. He paused and turned around to face me.

"Layung Cliffs. There is a long drop on the edge of the cliffs where idiots jump off in hopes of nose-diving into the water. Only about ten percent make it alive. The rest end up hitting their heads or worse on the rocks below."

I nodded, agreeing that Anthony's decision was a smart one.

When the Coast Guards find the body of Micah Henderson in the ocean, they would just assume he jumped off the cliff. It was an amazing idea.

"Alright, but be careful."

Anthony gave me a smirk, "Aren't I always?" He turned around and continued walking into the kitchen of Meryl Hopkins' five-bedroom brownstone, heading toward the backdoor where he parked his black car.

Shit! It's officially January 18th as it's 2:11 A.M.

Anthony and I spent hours cleaning up this entire house, making sure everything was how it was left. I haven't gotten any sleep and after seeing Micah's bludgeoned corpse upstairs; I don't think sleep is something I'm going to partake in for a while.

I made my way down the palace-like hallway into another living room decorated with old Victorian style paintings.

A fireplace was lit as it filled the room with an aroma of burning fabric that made me a little light headed. In the far-right corner was a glass case filled with three Tonys and five Emmy Award statuettes, along with three fashion dolls modeled after Meryl Hopkins' iconic eighteenth century dresses from the film *A Love Noir Of The Border.* As I saw, she keeps her five Oscar awards upstairs in a separate mantle by her bed.

Seated on the black leather sofa was the fifty-eight-year- old actress sipping a glass of whiskey. Her eyes laid on the crackling red and orange flames. She no longer had on the pink silk robe she visited me in, as that was the first thing I made her throw into the fireplace. Her long silver hair was in a fishtail braid that was slung over her right shoulder.

I had many philosophies in life that helped me get through difficult situations. Especially in my line of work, being able to find something to believe in was important. But one philosophy that always helped me was: Rip the band aid right off and never wait for the next ball to drop.

It was important for me to be twenty-five steps ahead of the game, because once you fall, Hollywood would waste no time trampling you and moving onto the next big thing. A sad, but true fact.

I walked into the room as quietly as I could, but the heels of my combat boots against the wooden floors announced me. "What the hell happened upstairs?"

The actress took her last sip of whiskey and turned away from the flames to look at me. "Have you ever been married, dahling?"

I didn't say anything, instead I responded with a slow nod.

"How long were you married for?"

"Three years." I muttered, hoping it was the last of that topic. Meryl gave me a simple nod and asked, "Why did it end?" The question caused me to sit on the armrest of another black sofa located just a few feet away from the one Meryl was seated on.

"We aren't here to talk about my personal life. I'm here helping you get away with murder and to clean up your mess! I'd like to get back on track and have you tell me what happened that made you snap and kill your husband."

She rose from the sofa and walked over to a mini bar located on the other side of the room. The actress wore a kimono that reminded me of the knock offs sold down by Fuller Road in downtown New Fran. I watched carefully as the woman poured herself another glass of whiskey.

"Micah was cast to play the role of Ian Sanders, a beggar that was going to die. My character, Elena, had only one scene with him, but...Micah won me over. He was just so mature when he spoke. So eloquent, that's a rarity nowadays. He's actually the only person I knew that could tell the difference between a painting by Manet and Monet."

I shifted on the armrest and watched Meryl down the whiskey as if it was water. She swallowed the whole drink without indicating that it was bitter.

"Anyway. He and I started speaking long after we finished filming. Every time he had an audition, he would confide in me and ask me for advice...It wasn't until a year later that he proposed to me. Proposed! A thirty-year-old man proposed to me, a woman in her fifties...can you imagine? I was taken aback, but I said yes. But we agreed to never tell the public about our marriage. That secret is the only thing that has kept us grounded."

"Okay, you got that off your chest. Now, tell me why he was lying in your bedroom with his head bashed in."

Meryl placed the empty glass down on the coffee table and she walked over toward the fireplace, where she stared at the hypnotic flames as if it was a siren singing to her.

"Micah came home the other day, drunk...he had never consumed alcohol before. At least not that I knew of. He was angry that I refused to pay him the money he wanted and he vowed to tell his agent everything about us. He was belligerent and I was frightened."

I lowered my eyebrows, listening to the words carefully. "Did he hit you?"

Meryl shook her head, "He never laid a finger on me in such a manner! He was just so angry and I tried to calm him down. I did. But then, he took my phone and threw it against the wall, smashing it into pieces. Which was why I went over to your office instead of calling you."

"What happened next?"

"Well, he grew angry that I didn't become upset when he broke my phone, so he started to talk about how he doesn't love me anymore because I'm old and disgusting. Then he said he hated me, because I would never be able to bear him a child."

I could tell those words cut Meryl deep as she started to reminisce about the incident.

I sensed the sadness in the woman's voice and I lowered my own, trying my hardest to sound sympathetic. "I know this is hard, Meryl, but I need you to tell me what happened next."

The woman turned around facing me. Her eyes were filled with tears of sadness and regret. "I got mad. Really mad. The only thing I could think about was causing those harsh words to stop echoing in the room...So I took my Oscar from the mantle and hit him over the head. Over and over again...until the room was filled with nothing but silence."

The emotions Meryl had been keeping inside were starting to crack the wall she had built up and she finally broke down, falling to her knees in sadness. "Oh my God! What have I done?! I killed my husband! The cops are going to find out and then I'm over. Done!"

"Anthony is going to dump Micah at Layung Cliffs and make it look like his death was accidental. I was able to call a few attorneys that owe me a favor. They helped sever all legal ties you and he had that could be traced back to you. Meaning any ventures you two had are expunged and gone. The marriage license as well. Anthony hacked his emails and he didn't find any mentions to close friends or family members about you two being together."

The words didn't do much to console Meryl at all. Sure, she was probably happy this couldn't be traced back to her, but at the same time she knew that she killed the only person she ever loved and now she had no one.

"Look, Meryl I can..."

"No!" The woman stated as she rose to her feet and dried her eyes. "I would like to be left alone. Is that alright?"

I didn't need much convincing. I gave Meryl a sincere smile and nodded. "No problem. But please, don't do anything else that you might regret." I grabbed my messenger bag and walked out of the living room.

I walked over to the front door and opened it, making my way down the stairs to the car, leaving Meryl crying in the living room in regret and sadness; and worst of all, guilt.

Chapter 9

My drive home was filled with a lot of emotions and thoughts invading my brain.

The day started out great at Ryan and Alice's wedding but then it took a weird turn when Salvatore showed up out of nowhere. Handling Jordan was a piece of cake so him trying to stir the pot wasn't anything I had to worry about. But Salvatore on the other hand, was a different story.

As soon as I got home, I took a hot shower to wash off the stress from the day.

Salvatore.

Micah's death.

Meryl's homicide.

And off topic, but I heard the private investigator, Oliver Morales, died in a car accident a few hours ago, after his car collided with a tractor trailer. Sure, I didn't wish him ill, but it was still sad to hear it as I literally saw this man the other day. However, I didn't have the time to mourn him, it was just too much.

The thoughts pertaining to Meryl and Micah were filled with guilt and pain. I kept blaming myself for refusing to go to dinner with the couple the other day. Maybe if I did go, I would've been able to see the signs that these two were not going to work out...but I didn't want to go because they were annoying me.

The constant flip flop of Meryl refusing to beat her husband at his own game gave me a headache that I really didn't want to bother with. Yet here I am now, sitting in my apartment after ordering dinner over the phone, ridden with guilt because Meryl killed her husband.

But once the train left from Meryl's station it moved onto Salvatore.

Why did the man I fell in love with years ago and who randomly wanted to divorce me, all of a sudden kiss me as if nothing happened?

As if he didn't break my heart? But worst of all? Why didn't I pull away from the kiss? Instead, I melted into his mouth as if I was a cup of ice cream on a heated radiator.

Knock! Knock! Knock!

I got up from the sofa wearing a long black shirt and a pair of tight briefs. I didn't feel like getting too dolled up for the delivery man because I wasn't in the mood. I just want to eat my food in the darkness and fall asleep; to awaken hours later, starting a brand-new day.

I unlocked the door to find a tall Cuban man holding my bag of food in his right hand and a smile on his face. "Hey Boots, I ran into the delivery guy and figured I would give the food to you, since I was heading this way anyways. I also tipped him ten bucks. So, you owe me ten bucks."

I shook my head glaring at Salvatore, "What the hell is wrong with you?"

"*Maldito bien!* You don't owe me."

"Not that, I'm talking about you divorcing me, then having the nerve to come back to my city to protect me from some psycho."

"*Ah bien. Así que veo que estamos haciendo esto.*" (Ah okay. So, I see we're doing this.).

"Damn right we are!"

Salvatore cleared his throat and clenched his jaws, "Fine, but can I at least come inside so we can do this in private?"

I stepped aside and opened the door wider, rolling my eyes.

Salvatore entered the apartment and I closed the door behind him, locking it.

"So, what do you want to know exactly?"

I turned around and Salvatore placed the bag filled with pancakes, bacon and eggs on the coffee table. "Uh, the part where you divorced me would be an amazing place to start."

He nodded his head and unzipped his black leather jacket as if he was trying to come up with an excuse to feed me.

"Alright. First things first, I didn't divorce you because I cheated. Let me clear the air on that."

"Oh, I know you didn't cheat. If you did, you wouldn't be walking around here with your penis still intact."

He sat down and I swore he grabbed his bulge as if he felt my words.

"I ended the marriage because…I was scared of losing you."

I frowned, not entirely sure what to make of that excuse.

How on earth was he going to lose me? "Um, yeah maybe you'd want to elaborate on that because I'm confused."

I sat down on the sofa next to him and he once again cleared his throat, "Look Boots, during that year our careers were excelling. I mean you and I were staying busy during the time the city shut down. *Fame Fixer Inc* was doing wonders and not to mention I was getting many politicians asking for my help in making them disappear." He took a deep breath and then continued again, "When I got notified about my clients all needing my help, I couldn't stop thinking about you. About how I was being a neglectful husband to you by constantly working and leaving you alone."

"I was never alone, Anthony was always here."

"Of course, he was." Salvatore scoffed, shaking his head.

I tilted my head, "What the hell is that supposed to mean?"

"Moving on." he interjected. "I knew that neglecting you would put us at odds with one another. I've seen it happen to my own parents, and look at them now. They hate each other. They can't even be in the same room during holidays without World War III taking place. I didn't want that to happen to us."

"And it wasn't. Not until you decided to end our marriage."

"I did it for us! I would rather have us end our marriage amicably than end up hating each other."

I waited to see if he was going to interject with a laugh or maybe a "sike!" but no, he just stopped talking and was clearly waiting for my reaction.

Once I saw he was done I decided to just say one word to sum up how I felt about that excuse he dropped on my lap, "Bullshit."

He frowned—clearly not what he was hoping for—and he said, "*¿Perdóneme?*" (Excuse me?)

I repeated the word and he jumped to his feet and started to pace back and forth.

"I can't believe you're sitting there and calling me a liar. *¡Un mentiroso! ¡Un narrador!* As if I would just make this up to hurt you."

"Oh no, I believe that was your reasoning. I do, but it's complete bullshit because I'm not some fragile China doll that you needed to protect. So what if our careers were causing us to drift apart and barely spend time with one another? Did you forget I fell in love with you because of your work ethics? I don't know what kind of guys you've met, but once I moved to this city, the guys I've met were not taking their careers seriously. You were the only man I met that had his shit together."

Did I fear once we got together, he would get super busy with his career and I would hardly see him? Not at all. I feared that he would cheat on me and leave me for someone younger. However, I knew space was great for Salvatore and I, so I never questioned when he had to work late or take a red eye to San Francisco in the morning. And he never questioned me when I would have to visit a client's house at two in the morning because she tweeted something racist after having a sugar high.

Yet when he told me that his parent's failed marriage is what caused him to have doubts about us, I knew it was complete and utter bullshit.

Salvatore sat back down on the sofa, letting out a sigh of frustration. I moved over and straddled his lap, looking at him calmly. "You need to understand Sal, I'm not weak. I'm not like any other guy out here who needs to cling to their man to feel loved. I trust you with all my heart and maybe that's a crazy thing to admit, but breaking news, I'm crazy. I have always loved you and yeah, maybe I wished your dick would fall off and a dog eats it..."

"Oww, okay maybe let's not bring Salvatore The Great into this," he said, placing his hands on my hips, and I couldn't help but laugh at him still calling his penis that.

"But I never stopped loving you," I continued. He licked his lips and glanced down at mine.

"Yeah?" he asked. "You never stopped?"

"If I did, you wouldn't be here right now."

He nodded, and placed his index finger on my lip.

I looked into his eyes as I wrapped my lips around his finger and started to suck on it slowly. I felt him get hard underneath. I slowly grinded on his lap moaning as his finger went down my throat as if it was his length.

He pulled his finger out of my mouth causing me to pout but little did I know he had a plan.

Salvatore used his left hand to pull my underwear down revealing my bare bottom. As he did this, he kept eye contact with me. I let out a gasp and leaned in closer to him as I felt that wet finger slowly enter inside of me.

"You're so tight." he whispered. His finger went in and out.

In and out.

I whimpered as his finger went further inside. The sensation is welcome after such a long time. I buried my face in the right side of his neck. He groaned in my ear and inserted another finger inside, challenging my tightness.

Why was he torturing me like this?

"Oh my God. My God." I moaned, arching my back, feeling myself stretch open as he pleasured me with his fingers. Minutes passed as I sat there, a moaning mess while my ex-husband fingered me, focusing solely on my pleasure. I was expecting him to whip out his length so I could ride him, but he didn't want me to.

Salvatore pushed the fingers deeper every time my entrance stretched wider. Not giving me any time to adjust, and honestly, I didn't want him to.

I was loving this!

Hell, I *needed* this.

I grabbed the back of his neck and started to bounce on his fingers, telling him not to pull out.

He slipped a third finger inside and that was it.

I let out a loud orgasm as I felt myself finished inside of my underwear.

My body twitched and I collapsed on him. Then he pulled his fingers out of me as I whimpered feeling myself tighten once again. "I could see you missed me," he said and I kissed his lips, laughing.

Pulling away from the kiss I looked up to meet his gaze, "So what does this mean?"

I wasn't sure if this was just a one-night stand, or if this was more. And everyone who knows me knows how much I hate the unknown.

"I'd like to think of this as the beginning of something new. Assuming you can handle me."

I laughed quietly at his words and kissed his lips, "I'm pretty sure *you're* the one that needs to worry about whether you can handle *me*."

"Oh really?" He gave my bottom a spank, which made me smirk and moan a little.

"I know I can handle you. But you might want to worry about my ex-husband. I hear he's *un fondo loco y sexy* (one crazy and sexy bottom)."

I cringed my nose at his words and playfully punched his arm, laughing.

I was laughing? Weird. It was definitely weird to hear myself laugh, genuinely again...very weird.

Chapter 10

January 18, 2023, at 8:16 A.M.
I stared at Anthony as he told me about a joke that made him laugh. My mind was occupied with the night I spent with Salvatore.

While we didn't have sex, it felt so nice to establish that emotional connection with him again. For us it was always emotional and less physical.

Knowing Anthony for as long as I have, I can tell when he wants to avoid a serious discussion because he cracks jokes that make no logical sense.

I let out a soft sigh and asked the question he probably didn't want to hear, "How's your mom?"

I could see the question hit him like a car, because he stopped talking and his eyes widened in shock.

Changing the subject would be the most logical thing for me to do, but I refused to leave that question hanging over our heads.

He gave me a slow nod and answered, "She's hanging in there. This is the second time she's battling breast cancer. Chemotherapy is kicking her ass, though. She's optimistic, like always but...Romero, I hate seeing her in pain."

Anyone who knew Anthony would describe him as a hard ass, headstrong and tough, but I knew other sides of him the world didn't. But in this moment, I saw the pain and frustration he was hiding from the world.

Anthony and his mother were also close, it's one of the many things I envied about him. His mother was there for him for his first crush, heartbreak, relationship, prom and whatever else heteros went through as teens.

Me? My mom died when I was young...all I had was my abuela, and don't get me wrong, she was strict and loving, but she wasn't my mother.

"But," Anthony continued, "she is planning a dinner this weekend and she wants you to come."

That invitation caused my heart to drop to the pit of my stomach for so many reasons, "Oh...she said that?"

He nodded, "Yeah, she actually insisted I tie you up and bring you there personally."

"I don't know Anthony, it would be too awkward for me to be there."

"Romero, she doesn't blame you. And she doesn't hate you. You're not at fault for what happened. You're innocent in all of this."

I opened my mouth to reply when I was cut off by the ringing of Anthony's phone. "Sorry." He took it out of his pocket and read the caller ID "It's my landlord. I'll take this outside."

Anthony walked out of my office and just like God working her strange magic, my office phone began to ring as well.

I quickly picked it up, "Romero."

"Good morning, Jayson Romero! My name is Todd Phillips and I am calling because I want to inquire about your services." The man's tone was calm and very professional, as if he was a public speaker.

"Oh, of course. What's the problem?"

"I'm sorry, Jayson, but I do not feel comfortable discussing this over the phone," he replied.

I understood.

Not many of my clients feel their phones are safe enough to discuss private matters, so they always want to meet up in person to discuss their problems.

"Alright, that's totally understandable. Is there a day or time you're free?"

"I'm free right now, if you are."

"I'm actually free right now as well."

"Great! I'm located at 3266 Arlane Road. I'll see you soon." The man hung up the phone and I did the same.

Why the hell did that address sound so familiar to me?

I don't know, but I'm about to find out.

• • • •

<u>TEN MINUTES LATER:</u>

Arlane Road is one of the busiest roads here in New Fran. It's home to boutiques of famous designers that sell their clothes and items starting from six thousand dollars and onward. It's just ugly fabric that people need to purchase because their favorite celebrity wore it in a photoshoot. Bleh!

I was just happy to find a parking spot on a Wednesday morning. Thank God the boutiques open at noon.

I walked to the front of 3266 Arlane Road, and shook my head, "Son of a bitch!"

The building in front of me was a church known as *The New Hope of Samson's Latter Days*, a church famous throughout New Fran City for their clients who tend to be huge A- List Hollywood stars. The church only admitted men as it followed the belief that men are the divine souls of God and women are just beings God created to bear children with.

They are not allowed to marry or be in a relationship with a woman because doing so will cause them to lose sight of their spiritual paths that God had laid out before them.

The founder of this cult religion was Roger Meldore. He created this church to teach men the story of Samson and Delilah.

I let out a sigh and approached the glass door. I was impressed when it opened automatically. Walking through the threshold, I was met with a large gold and white colored lobby that looked more like a hotel lobby than a church.

A man no older than twenty-six smiled at me as I approached the large white and golden desk he was seated behind. "Good morning, my fellow brother. My name is Ezekiel, how are you feeling today?"

"Well considering I didn't burst into flames once I passed the threshold, I'd say I'm doing fine." I smiled back and he looked at me as if I was speaking gibberish.

I didn't expect him to get my dark sense of humor.

I cleared my throat and continued, "I'm Jayson Romero and I'm here to see Todd Phillips."

"Ah yes! Pastor Todd Phillips said he was expecting you. Please wait while I call him." He picked up the golden painted phone and dialed the number one, he gave me that same painted smile as he placed the phone on his right ear. "Hello Pastor Phillips. Jayson Romero is here to see you. Yes, I'll let him know." He hung up the phone and looked at me. "He will be here shortly."

"Okay, thank you." I didn't really know what else to say to this man.

Pastor Todd Phillips? Did I do something in my past life that God is now punishing me for by having me here? I mean seriously.

Before I could tap my feet awkwardly on the floor, Ezekiel asked "So, how big is your package?"

I frowned at his question and paused to make sure I heard the question correctly. "I'm sorry...what?"

"Your package. Here at New Hope, we have different size packages that we offer our members. The Large package gets you two free months at the local gym and any events New Hope hosts. The Extra-Large package gets you six free months. The Double Extra-Large package gets you three years of free gym access."

I smirked at the male, "Oh Ezekiel, no one likes a size queen."

Ezekiel opened his mouth to say something but he was interrupted by a clapping sound that came from a taller man who walked down the hallway, wearing a very tightly buttoned up shirt and khaki pants. "Good morning. You must be Jayson Romero. I'm Pastor Todd Phillips." The tall man extended his right hand at me.

I shook his hand and gave it a firm squeeze because I loathed everything this church was teaching to the city. And as a fixer, I cannot show my bias.

The Pastor took his hand back, "Let's head to my office so we can discuss the reason why I summoned you down here."

He walked down the hallway and Ezekiel whispered to me, "You should get the Double Extra-Large package from him." I

gave him a smirk and whispered back, "I have a feeling neither he nor you have the Double Extra-Large packages that I would like to take." I gave him a wink and followed the Pastor who continued to walk down the hall.

"I hope you aren't too offended being here, Brother Romero." Todd stated as we continued walking down the large hallway that looked like an exhibit inside of a museum that was a tribute to royalty.

"Please call me Jayson ." I replied.

"Oh, is Brother Romero discourteous?"

"Not at all. It's just not very professional." I didn't want the man to get used to calling me that in hopes of trying to coax me to whatever kind of backward fraternity this church is.

We made it to a golden colored door and he opened it. "Please sit and we can discuss the situation at hand."

I nodded and made my way over to a black leather chair that was seated across from his unnecessarily large desk. The office window overlooked the New Fran river. I had no idea the river was literally on the other side. I couldn't help but wonder how big this church really was.

Todd closed the door and made his way over toward his throne sized chair, sat down, took out a manila colored envelope from the inside of his desk drawer, placed it in front of him on the desk and smiled at me as he folded his hands together in front of him.

"The reason I called you over here is because I'm afraid a sheep has strayed from the flock."

"No offense, Pastor, but that sounds like an Ace Ventura problem."

Silence.

I'm giving my best comical material today and no one is laughing or cracking a smile! I know the men who are part of this cult, give up thousands of dollars every month, but did they give up their sense of humor, too?

Todd continued, "His name is Pastor Jason Todd, he is one of the brightest stars in this congregation. He has brought in close to sixty million dollars in two months for this church."

I nodded, listening to his words closely, "Glad to see it's all about faith with you." I replied sarcastically and I'm sure he caught on to that because he slid the folder toward me.

"One of my brightest stars is close to dimming, Brother Romero. Apparently, there's a wolf who's digging their claws into my sheep and I cannot have that."

I opened the folder to be met with countless pictures of a man who looked like he could double as Chris Pine, having sex with a Latina woman in the backseat of a black car parked in an alleyway. The photos were taken with a very high-definition camera, because these pictures were as clear as day! Clearly, this photographer wasn't a professional paparazzi, as none of them in New Fran City have cameras this amazing.

"The Jezebel in the photo is Carmen Lopez. She's an adult film actress. Are you familiar with her work?"

I glared up at the Pastor and asked, "Do you honestly believe I'm familiar with the work of a female adult actress?"

He nodded and continued, "She and Jason had been sending emails to each other for weeks leading up to this perverse indiscretion."

"Um, no offense Todd—"

"Pastor Todd." He corrected and all I could do at this point was nod and smile, a very painful smile as I held back what I originally wanted to say.

"Yeah sure." I continued, "If this indiscretion, as you call it, is something you knew about, then why am I here looking at pictures that you conveniently hid in a folder, when you can talk to Jason yourself?"

"I didn't take these pictures. I received them last night from a mysterious person. They demanded fifty million dollars in cash to be hand delivered to them by noon tomorrow. I would've gone to the police but it doesn't take a genius to know what New Fran City thinks about my church and its message."

He's referring to the misogyny and homophobia this church has displayed on numerous occasions in the past. Not just privately, but also very publicly.

I agreed with Todd, photos like these would've had their enemies trying to sell them to the highest bidder.

"I get why you didn't want to go to the cops. But why not pay the ransom? I mean after all, Jason Todd is like your church brother."

"Brother Romero, money is very vital to New Hope. It's the heartbeat that gives this church life. Surely, you're insane if you think I'm going to give the church's money away to some extortionist because Jason wasn't strong enough to avoid the grips of a succubus."

Oh yeah, I forgot at *New Hope of Samson* a woman is seen as being a succubus. Apparently, they took the tale of Samson and Delilah and retold it to their congregation. In their new version, God created men and Satan created women to emasculate, seduce and dethrone men. Yet they seek women out to conceive children with them in hopes of raising an army that will be strong enough to defeat Satan and his mistresses. It's all very confusing.

"So, you want me to speak to Jason and make all of this go away?"

"Not quite." Todd stated as he leaned back in his chair, getting comfortable. "I need you to prep him for his interview once these photos go viral."

"You're going to leak them?" I was completely taken aback with what I just heard.

"Like I said, I'm not going to give in to the demands of some blackmailer. Because of this, I expect the pictures to go viral and I encourage everyone to see them. So, they can all be awakened with the fact that women are temptresses that need to be tamed."

Todd was just another run of the mill misogynist who used his religion to justify his hatred toward women. One day I would love to know his secrets, instead, I have to focus on Jason Todd and Carmen Lopez.

Todd continued, I think this time he was talking about aliens. I don't honestly know because I was tuning him out. I was looking over the pictures of Jason and Carmen and I couldn't help but notice the car changes between each picture as well as the location of the alleyway.

These two have been meeting in secret for a long time, it was obvious this wasn't their first rodeo. But as I made my way down to the last picture in the deck, I saw something I hadn't seen in a long time.

The picture in question had Carmen sitting on Jason's lap and they were staring into each other's eyes. Jason and Carmen aren't in a sexual encounter with each other, they're in—

"Love." I said, completely unaware I was thinking aloud until Todd nodded.

"Exactly! Love is what these women use to dig their poisonous claws into the flesh of men."

"Oh sorry, I didn't realize you were still talking." I muttered as I got up from the seat. "Where can I find Jason?"

"He has a room in the Shelont Motel, ten minutes away from here. He's in room 1C."

I frowned, "A motel? I would think communal living would be a lot cheaper than an old crusty motel."

Todd smiled, "He has betrayed the teachings of the word, so he will spend his time at a motel until we can get this situation under control, or better yet, until *you* can get this situation under control."

"Okay, great." I flashed him one of my infamous fake smiles. "Can I keep the pictures? Not for personal reasons, but to show them to Jason?"

Todd waved his right hand, dismissing me. "Do as you must. Just get him ready for war. Carmen started this and we're going to finish it."

I nodded, not bothered by his threat, and left the office with the manila folder tucked underneath my right arm.

I made my way down the hallway quickly and I cursed every step I took as my steel-toed boots kept making clunking noises on the shiny tiled floor.

"I hope you had a great time here at New Hope and remember, you too can be the top of your faith. Just like me." The secretary said through his obnoxious smile.

"Something tells me, just like myself, you're not a top." I replied, and I was met with a blank expression.

I gave Ezekiel a wink and continued to walk toward the automatic doors without letting any step slow me down.

Finally outside, I stopped walking and let the New Fran City wind just blow away any and all negativity I had.

It was my first time stepping foot in New Hope of Samson and I already felt dirty, angry and disgusted by their beliefs.

"You're leaving a church in one piece?" I heard a familiar voice ask and I looked over to see Anthony leaning on a parked car. "No flames? Huh. Either you're secretly a good boy or God is really sleeping on you."

I looked at Anthony, unsure of what to think or say after my encounter with Todd.

He smirked at me, "I went into your office to get some staples because I ran out and I saw the address on your notepad. I knew this address by hand because well, New Hope has a reputation. I thought either you'd burn the place down or maybe they would try something stupid. So, I figured I'd come down here to make sure you were okay."

I listened to every word Anthony said. "Well, I'm glad you're here. I was seconds away from losing my crap back there. This place is something else."

Anthony nodded and pointed to the folder under my arm. "What's that? Please tell me you didn't take his package."

I smirked at Anthony. "If I did, Pastor Todd would be worshiping *me*."

Anthony chuckled. Finally, someone who laughed at my joke!

"No. He hired me for a job. I'll fill you in, while you drive us to the motel."

Anthony stared at me, "Wait, what now?"

I gave him my car keys because I wasn't really in the mood to drive and I needed to focus on this interesting case at hand.

Chapter 11

T<u>en minutes later:</u>

The drive to the Shelont Motel was much longer than I anticipated. Then again, I had my assistant driving and he's clearly better at firing a weapon than driving.

When we arrived in the parking lot of the motel he parked my car in a parking spot that was a few feet away from room 1C. The same room where Pastor Jason Todd called home for the time being.

On the drive over, I showed Anthony the pictures and explained the situation to him. "Sounds to me like good ol' New Hope would lose a lot if those images got out."

"Yet strangely, he doesn't want to stop them from circulating. He's against the idea of paying the blackmailer off, which is understandable, but he wants these images out there for everyone to see."

Anthony turned the car off, leaned back on the driver's seat and looked at me with concern on his face. "So why did you agree to take this on? You're not the type to let things like this leak to the press. You're the one that tries to stop it."

"Because of this." I pulled out the picture of Carmen and Jason gazing into each other's eyes.

"I don't get it." Anthony replied, staring at it.

"Ugh! Of course, a hetero man wouldn't." I shook my head, "Love! That look in their eyes isn't some mammal sexual gaze. It's love, trust me, I used to know that look. I used to give that look."

I didn't want to spend any more of my time talking about or thinking about Salvatore...not yet anyway.

"Alright." He handed me the picture. "What's the plan? New Hope wants you to have Jason blame the sexual encounters on Carmen?"

"That's why I wanted to see him away from the church. If he can tell me that he loves Carmen and she loves him, I can spin this entire narrative and blame New Hope for the pictures leaking. It won't ruin much of Jason's reputation. Although he may lose the crowd of incels that worship him."

"And you're ready to take on an organization like New Hope? They might have some big guns aimed at you."

I met Anthony's eyes and arched my right eyebrow at him, "I already have some crazy person dumb enough to put a bounty on my head. If New Hope wants me dead, they're going to have to take a number and get in line," I replied with a smirk on my face.

Anthony once again nodded and I noticed a car a few feet away from us that was parked as well. It was a gold Nissan that looked to be outdated, the doors were rusted, dirty and the windows were tinted.

I knew exactly who that car belonged to and it sickened me to see them here. *"¡Hijo de puta!"* I unclipped my seatbelt, pushed the passenger door open and stormed over to the other car.

I didn't want to make a scene in the parking lot that would alert Jason, but thankfully the crappy gold car was parked away from room 1C.

I knocked on the black tinted window of the driver's side. "Open up, I know you're in there. I can smell the scent of failure and bourbon." I said.

The window rolled down and revealed a middle-aged pudgy and greasy looking man. His name is Trevor Cawell. He runs the largest tabloid magazine in New Fran City called *Daily Whispers*. "Oh, hey Jasmine! How are you?"

"What the hell are you doing here?"

The man smirked at me. "I assume you're here to put out the bag of feces someone lit on fire and dumped on New Fran City's front step?"

There was no doubt in my mind that he was referring to Pastor Jason Todd's scandal. But I sure as hell wasn't going to tell him that I knew anything.

So, I opted to act like celebrities when they tweet something racist and get fired from a hit TV show; play dumb.

"What are you talking about?" I asked.

"Don't pretend that New Hope isn't running things in the city. Who do you think is kidnapping teenagers? You don't seriously believe that twenty-three teens ran away from home in the last week, do you? No! I put all my money that New Hope is kidnapping teenage girls to impregnate them."

I frowned, listening to the words coming out of Trevor's mouth. He might be a slime ball who once wrote about how the First Lady of the country is secretly an alien from Neptune, and that story had news coverage for months! But when it comes to religious organizations, I know there is something dirty taking place in all of them. Maybe he was right, but this was something that wasn't in my field. "So why are you camping out here where Jason Todd is hiding out?"

"Because I know Jason isn't part of New Hope's recruitment of teens. In fact, I have reasons to believe that he wants out and is willing to talk to someone about the truth."

"And you think you're the best person for him to talk to?" Anthony asked as he walked over to us.

"Yeah, I do. Isn't that why you're here? To take them down, too? Or are you working for them?"

I rolled my eyes at that offensive question, "Not that it's any of your business but I'm here to get to the bottom of something. I think it's best if you leave."

"Best if I leave?" I didn't expect Trevor to come out of his car—mainly because I wasn't expecting him to be wearing pants—so when he did it shocked me.

"I need to send New Hope a message and us sitting on our asses as they spread lies about the world, especially your community, isn't going to help anyone when they are destroying us!"

There was something in Trevor's voice that caught me off guard; it was full of hurt and pain.

"What did they do to you?" I asked slowly.

Trevor shook his head and ran his hands through his thin black hair. "They killed my son...I mean daughter. She was transgendered and I was coming to terms with who she was, but New Hope got to her first and fed her a bunch of lies that she was making a fool of the family name and they lied to her saying she was sick. I was shocked when she came out and a bit confused, but I accepted her because I love her and that's what a real parent does...But that meant nothing to her, New Hope already made her think I was disgusted by her. She killed herself last week...she was only sixteen years old."

"I...I'm so sorry." Was all that I could muster because I didn't know he had a child or let alone one that was part of the LGBT community.

He dismissed my words, "I don't want to hear condolences until I bring down New Hope."

I decided to do something that I would probably regret, but I didn't care at this point, because this cult needed to be stopped.

I walked away from Anthony and Trevor and headed back to my car where I took out the manila folder and I walked back over to Trevor. "You are to make sure you go public with this after I call you tonight. I need to get Jason and Carmen on the same page."

I handed him the folder and he opened it to look at the pictures. "Are you sure about this? This could destroy Jason."

"What better way to hit back at New Hope than to show the public how cruel their leader is to try and get in the way of true love?"

"You think these two are in love?"

"That's what we're going with. Start the cover page but like I said, do not post anything until I get Jason and Carmen on board and then we can give you the exclusive interview."

He nodded, "I was wrong about you, Jasmine—I mean Jayson."

I gave him a wink, "Most people are."

He got back inside of his car and closed the door.

"I don't mean to question you Romero, but are you sure that was a good idea?" Anthony asked me.

The golden Nissan pulled out of the parking lot and drove down the empty street. "I don't know. Ask me that again tomorrow morning."

I refocused on why I was here at the seedy motel. We headed toward room 1C. I knocked on it lightly. After a few seconds, I heard a man laughing from the other side of the door, "Did you forget the key?" and the door opened to reveal a tall middle-aged man with short dirty blond hair and hazel eyes.

I gave him a smile as he looked at Anthony and I as if we were unwanted guests. "Good morning. My name is Jayson Romero and this tall man behind me is my assistant. We're here because I was hired by Pastor Todd Phillips to speak with you about your relations with Carmen Lopez."

Jason's face turned pale, but he opened the door wider, gesturing for us to come in. We entered the room and I was impressed. For a rundown motel, the room had two beautifully made beds, a mural of something that looked like an ocean wave carrying a...shark? A huge plasma television screen and even a kitchen that was stocked with fresh fruits. This motel sure changed from when I was here with Salvatore many years ago.

"I don't mean to sound rude," Jason said as he closed the door, and I turned to look at him. "But why did Todd Phillips send you?"

"Well, I'm a fixer for high profile people. Your boss had informed me that you and Ms. Lopez have been pictured on numerous occasions having sex in a few cars that usually tend to be parked in alleys."

The Pastor shook his head and asked nervously, "P- pictures?"

I nodded. "It seems that whomever took those pictures is currently blackmailing New Hope for fifty million dollars. Pastor Todd has made it abundantly clear that he is not obliging and he refuses to be extorted for money that belongs to the church. So, the blackmailer will be leaking these photos to the public tomorrow at noon."

"No, no, no." Jason began to pace back and forth and Anthony sat on the edge of a faux wooden dresser that was located by the door.

"You're here to fix this situation? I mean, I don't even know how you can fix something like this, and..." He stopped pacing and asked me with concern and fear in his voice, "And Todd said he wouldn't pay off the blackmailer?"

I nodded again and he shook his. "I knew that scumbag was too good to be true. Now I'm going to be ruined!"

"Actually, you're not," I replied and he let out a chuckle.

"Yeah, right."

"I'm serious, Mr. Todd. I saw those pictures of you and Carmen. In one of those frames, you two were staring into each other's eyes and I saw something there. I saw love. The church probably saw that too, which is why they're panicking and ready to throw you to the wolves so you can fend for yourself. But I'm here to make sure your story is told."

"My story? I'm not sure where you're looking, but my story is going from respectable Christian leader to sexual deviant in less than twenty-four hours."

"Actually, it's not," I stated. "As I said, I saw love in your eyes. And I can assume you're in this motel because it's the only place where you and Carmen can meet and be in each other's company without having the church or anyone else down your necks?"

He nodded his head slowly. "Yeah, it is."

"Exactly. I can help you two come out to the public as a couple. A modern-day Romeo and Juliet minus the underage sex and poorly executed fake double suicide."

Jason opened his mouth, but his words were cut short when the door to the room opened and in walked Carmen Lopez, holding a brown paper bag from Eddy's Diner.

If anyone visits New Fran City, they must eat at Eddy's Diner. They make the best flapjacks known to man, woman or whatever you identify as.

Carmen closed the door looking at Anthony, who waved at her, and then she turned to look at me as she walked into the kitchen, placing the deliciously smelling food on the counter. "Uh, what's going on?"

I didn't want to spend more time going over the reason why I'm here again, so I recapped the situation to her by explaining how the church hired me to make her look like a succubus. I also explained that because I noticed the look of love between them, I knew instantly that I wanted to spin this story to make them two look like a modern-day Romeo and Juliet.

Carmen smiled and looked at Jason, "Do you think with Jayson 's help we can finally live happily ever after?"

Jason smiled at her and he pushed a strand of black hair away from her face and nodded, "I want to believe so, sweetheart." He touched her stomach and smiled wider, "For all three of our sakes."

"You're pregnant?" I gasped.

Carmen nodded, smiling in excitement. "Yep, just a few weeks."

"Great!" I said as I clapped my hands together. "We can have you two make a video post where you're talking about how much in love you two are in and then Jason can admit to the church's mistreatment of him because—"

Carmen interrupted my plan and she said she was very grateful for me helping but she's currently hungry and needs to eat something.

"Can I come back in ten minutes?" I asked.

She nodded along with Jason. "That sounds like a plan." I left the room with a smile on my face, but that smile slowly faded away when I realized that although everything seemed to be going in a positive direction in my work life; my personal life was a dumpster fire that not even water can put out.

I walked over to my car and sat on the hood.

Anthony exited the room, closing the door behind him and followed me. "Is everything okay, Romero?"

I nodded and smiled at him. He wasn't buying it. No matter what I said, he wasn't going to buy it.

I can manipulate the world, but when it comes to Anthony, I could never lie to him because he sees through it. I'm not sure if that's a blessing or a curse.

I let out a sigh and shook my head.

He walked over to the hood and sat down next to me. "What's going on in that brain of yours?"

"I'm going to be thirty in two days," I replied. My voice wasn't loud enough for anyone in the rooms to hear, and although there were at least six other cars parked in the parking lot, no one else but us were out and about.

"Are you seriously complaining about that?"

I nodded, "Yes! You know how much I loathe that day."

"*That* day? That day is your birthday. It's a blessing that you are able to celebrate another year. Most people aren't so lucky."

"Oh, cut that Disney crap out! Ever since I was born, I've learned the hard way that my birthday is cursed."

"Cursed? How?"

Was he serious? It was on my first birthday that my mother died. I never saw my birthday as a reason to celebrate after my mother saw it as a day to kill herself.

On my sixteenth birthday, my abuela got me a brand-new car, which was crushed by a tree that fell on it. I didn't even get a chance to drive it down the street!

On my eighteenth birthday, my apartment was broken into and my laptop, phone and jewelry were stolen.

On my twenty-first birthday, I got food poisoning.

And on my twenty-eighth birthday, my husband decided to divorce me.

So yeah, I don't think my birthday is a day for me to celebrate, but rather a day for me to hide from the world.

"Are you really going to ignore your birthday as if it's Father's Day?"

"Yes, and Yes," I retorted without wasting any seconds.

"That's insane! You're turning thirty years old! That's a huge milestone. You can't just sit at your office all day and ignore it."

"I'm turning thirty and what do I have to show for it? I'm currently having an affair with my ex-husband who's back in the city–"

"Wait, what?" Anthony asked, and I realized that I blurted out something that should've been a thought.

But I continued anyways, "Not to mention I have someone who wants me dead and will pay half of ten million dollars to see it happen. I can't celebrate something like this when I don't feel like I deserve to."

Anthony jumped off the hood of the car and stood in front of me. "We're going to circle back to the whole you're still seeing Salvatore, later. But are you serious right now? You don't deserve to? You saved me, Romero! If it wasn't for you, I wouldn't be here right now."

"Bullshit."

"Nah, it isn't!" Anthony stated, "Being a hired hitman paid a hell of a lotta money. And being able to travel to various cities and countries was amazing. But when my mom was diagnosed with breast cancer...I had to quit. I didn't know what I would do with myself. I hated everything for what was happening to my ma, and I was honestly about to give up. Yet I didn't, because she needed me."

I didn't know what to say when Anthony shared that story. He wasn't really one to get too deep into his emotions and share anything about his family. I'm not sure if that's an Anthony thing or a heterosexual man's thing. Either way, seeing this side of Anthony was brand-new.

"And then you hired me to be your assistant. The pay is so much better than my last job and here I am five years later. I'm able to see my mom daily, check in on her and eat her homemade mondongo every Saturday."

I sighed, remembering how delicious her mondongo is, "I do love mondongo."

"Exactly. You may not feel like you've accomplished much, but you have."

I heard my phone ring and forgot I left it on the dashboard of the car. I hopped off the hood and opened the driver's door to grab it. The caller ID read Unknown Number and although I had no idea who the hell could be calling, I figured I would answer it anyways.

"Hello, this is Romero," I answered.

"Good morning, Jayson , this is Pastor Todd Phillips."

"Oh, hello. I was about to call you."

"That's quite insightful. I'm calling because I don't think you and I are on the same page about the situation at hand. It seems you are determined to run your own agenda that differs from that of New Hope of Samson."

I didn't understand what he was talking about. "I don't understand. You hired me to do a job and that's what I'm trying to do."

"I don't believe it's the way that I would like for you to do it. I'm sorry, but you're fired. I hope you enjoy the rest of your day."

He hung up the phone on his end and I looked at mine in confusion.

"What happened?" Anthony asked.

"Todd fired me. He said that my agenda didn't match the agenda of his church."

"Well, that's crazy. What you're doing is telling the truth."

"Exactly, and clearly he doesn't see it that way, but—wait a minute. How did he know what I was doing? He couldn't have known unless he had ears in that room."

"So, you think he's spying on us?"

"No." I paused and thought about what Todd said. Then I realized the unthinkable, "I think there was someone else in the room."

I ran over to door 1C and turned the knob, but it was locked. "Jason, it's me! Open this door!" I shouted as I slammed my hands against the door.

"Here, watch out." Anthony took out a small black gun with a silencer on the tip from the inside of his designer jacket and I quickly moved back as he aimed it at the doorknob. He pulled the trigger and the knob flew right off.

I pushed the door open and paused in shock as I saw the dead bodies of Carmen and Jason Todd on the ground.

"Son of a bitch." I knelt and saw they were dead from gunshot wounds.

"This was a hit!" Anthony ran over to the bathroom.

I tried to stupidly find a pulse on either Carmen or Jason but they were too far gone. Both were shot in the head, assassination style.

Carmen stared up to the ceiling and Jason was flat on his stomach. Their food was still in the paper bag.

"Whoever killed them is long gone." Anthony said, walking out of the bathroom in anger. "The window leads to an alleyway just north of here."

I shook my head and got up from the floor.

"They were killed right after we left. Todd had someone here waiting for them...they were waiting for us to leave so they could shut these two up."

Anthony placed the gun back in his jacket. "Jason was the sheep that strayed far away from the herd."

"No." I replied looking at Anthony. "He was the sacrificial lamb."

I pulled out my cellphone to dial 911, but I paused and realized there was a bigger story here, one that wouldn't be enough for me to dive into, but one that I can sure as hell assist in.

I dialed a number and placed the phone on my ear as the other line began to ring.

"Hello?"

"Trevor, it's me, Jayson."

"Ah, perfect! I'm at the office now. Are we set up to destroy New Hope?"

"There's been a slight change in plans, and this new change will definitely help boost your credentials."

I looked back over at the bodies and sighed in frustration. I didn't know them well enough to mourn them, but I did know they were in love. That love was what made a man leave his cult and that same love was set to produce a baby, a baby that will never get to see the light of day now.

Carmen and Jason were products of a cult that saw money before faith. It's that same cult that needs to be exposed for what they did and I'm glad to be the man that helps make that happen!

Chapter 12

<u>**January 19, 2023, at 8:25 P.M.**</u>

Tori Lane stared angrily into the camera as the caption '*Tori's Talk Time*' slid across the screen under her image. Her signature platinum blonde hair was more yellow on the screen and her fake tanned skin more orange. What the hell is going on with the network's color balance?

"I'm sure now that the presidential election has winded down, liberals are still big crybabies about the results. They are causing mayhem on the streets by protesting and stopping traffic. They are destroying their own communities. Leave it to the libtards to mess up the economy and blame it on republicans. Which is amusing as there wouldn't have been an election if the previous president had kept his penis in his pants. He wouldn't have had to resign after being caught with his whore." She shook her head in disgust and continued speaking.

"One libtard in particular, is Korean-turned English pop singer, Geo Kionè. He spent a majority of the campaign bashing Presidential Elect Reber at every chance he got. Well, his act took a comical turn when he performed on another liberal show, 'Comedy Sketch Laugh Live' last night and he suffered technical difficulties. Instead of him performing like a true artist, he ended up cursing the producers, cast and crew, his fans, the mayor and even the president.

What I don't get about these Hollyweird Show Ponies is who gives them a right to talk politics? Who are they to even share their opinion on the happenings of this amazing nation? They don't even work hard! Instead, they go to the studio, read lines off a page, and get paid to be the face of whatever pathetic cosmetic line hires them!

I have a long list of problems with Hollyweird libtards, believe me, but my real issue is with Geo Kionè. This is a man who spent a majority of his career singing Korean pop songs. He was made a United States citizen two years ago, and he thinks he knows what is good for this nation?

His rant once again proves why the president needs to focus his energy on withdrawing from any ties with the Asian nations! He's a disgrace to Korea and most importantly a disgraceful American that needs to have his citizenship revoked ASAP!"

I muted the television screen in my office and swiveled in my office chair to face Geo Kionè.

He was seated on the chair across from my desk and he couldn't believe what he just heard.

"Is she serious?" he asked nervously.

"I wouldn't entertain her opinion," I stated.

"But what now? That video went viral and every social media blog has dubbed me difficult to work with. I'm far from that. I didn't mean to say anything offensive. I just had a crazy night. The microphone wasn't working and none of the stage hands were helping. Clearly, they were sabotaging me for ratings. Which they got because that video of me cursing everyone out, has gotten over six million views."

He wasn't lying about that. If he thought the views were extreme, he should read the comment section. That was ten times worse.

I grabbed the tablet off my desk and swiped the screen, trying to find the video that Geo was referring to. After a few searches, I was able to find it on the media app Me-Tube. I turned the tablet over so the screen faced Geo and pressed the play button.

The Korean singer combed his fingers through his neon- colored green hair and watched the video as it played.

In the video Geo strums a few strings of his neon-green acoustic guitar, playing a beautiful but sad tune, and sings a few words into the microphone. He closes his eyes as he continues strumming each string and he finally opens them to gaze into the camera as the audience of women screams his name at the top of their lungs.

"Ooooh, where did you spend the night, my love?

Ooooh, I gave my heart, was that enough?

Noooow, I lay here bl-ing f—while you—st—"

Geo stops singing, but continues to play the guitar, hoping someone behind the scenes heard the microphone disrupting his vocals. He clears his throat and continues singing, realizing no one was coming to help him.

"But you! You lied to me with the same lips that kissed me! The same lips that—made—i-S—Fine—mi—loaded—"

Finally having enough, Geo stops playing the guitar, slams it onto the floor of the stage, breaking it into pieces as the crowd stops cheering and looks at him in shock.

"I am tired of this Bleeping country! Thinking you can just Bleep me over and that's okay? Bleep ComedyTV! Bleep America! And Bleep Reber!"

Without saying another word, Geo storms off the stage, leaving his fans shocked at his behavior and hurt.

I stopped the video and placed the tablet back on my desk as Geo buried his face in his hands in embarrassment.

"I...I don't know what to say. I look like a total jackass! My fans must hate me."

"Actually, they don't. According to the hashtag they created called #WeStandWithGeo, they haven't left your side."

Geo felt at ease to know his fans didn't fully abandon him, but it didn't give him one hundred percent hope as many of the future gigs he was booked for were canceled. They feared he would flip out on them as well if technical difficulties arose.

"I love my fans, Mr. Romero. I truly do. I get that I screwed up badly. But I need you to fix this. Make all of this go away! I came to America to extend my music career, not to be destroyed by an angry outburst."

I could see the sadness in Geo's eyes and hear the passion in his voice. I opened the drawer to my desk, took out a flier and handed it to him.

He took the flier and read it, frowning. "What's a Flango Mango?"

"That's the new bar which opened on Eighth Avenue last year. The bar has an open mic with a culturally diverse clientele. I'm talking about cosplayers, hipsters and LGBT individuals. These people go there to enjoy the scenery and music and I believe you performing there will give you a redo of all of this."

Geo couldn't help but notice the flier had his face on it, with the specific time and place that he was performing, and oddly enough, the date of his performance was tonight!

Yes, I didn't run anything by him or his record label, but they weren't doing anything to help him because they were too busy trying to replace him with another individual, just like Tommy Mottola replacing Mariah Carey with Jennifer Lopez.

He shook his head and placed the flier down on my desk. "I didn't approve of any of this."

I nodded slowly. "I know you didn't. I did. You see, you are going to perform here because this is a gig. Something you and I both know isn't really available to you since your little Christian Bale meltdown. Now, the show starts tonight at one A.M. sharp. You will focus on the next four hours writing a new song that you will debut during your open mic showcase tonight."

"A new song?" Geo gasped. "You must be crazy! I cannot write a song in almost four hours. That's crazy, especially for me!"

"You will write a new song, preferably about being cheated on, because you are going to apologize to your fans for your behavior last night. You will tell them that you found your girlfriend having sex with your best friend. You thought that you could handle it, but the technical issues you suffered caused every emotion you had to come flooding back at once. This excuse will paint you as the victim and you will win the hearts of every man, woman, enby, child and teen!"

Geo had to admit the idea was genius. It gave him an excuse for his behavior although he was angry at the station, but it helped ease his scandal.

"I also hired a private investigator and she's going to be looking into the security tapes from the studio yesterday to see if there was any sabotage that screwed your performance over."

Geo smiled. "So, you also believe the studio screwed me?"

"Right now, it's too early to say anything, but if that is proven correct, I will leak this information to the public, which will ultimately sever all ties with the studio and your record label."

I could tell Geo didn't care about whether or not his label would approve of this decision if the truth was exposed. The only thing he cared about was his reputation and his career. "Okay, that sounds good. My label would be happy to hear I'm working on a new song."

I smiled and nodded. "Sounds great. I'll be there and you don't need to worry about your fans, they'll show up. Remember, if any technical issues do happen, you are to continue with your performance. Fans love nothing more than when an artist continues singing while suffering tech issues, remember that."

Geo gave me a nod, stood and walked out of the office, probably feeling so much better than when he came in.

I watched as he left the office, making his way toward the hallway, and walked over toward my office phone. I dialed a number and listened as it began to ring on the other line.

After three rings, the line was picked up and I heard a disgruntled voice greet me.

"Hello Marvin, it's Jayson Romero."

"Ah, the fixer! How bad is it? Is Geo's reputation salvageable or do I have to cut him loose like a gold-digging ex-wife?"

The fact his first thoughts were on Geo's reputation rather than the singer's mental health explains the current state of this industry.

While I'm only hired to fix my client's reputation, I tend to care a bit about what made that client act out the way they did. Or say what they said that got them—as the guys with neckbeards would say—canceled.

I tried to do this with Joe and Lola, but that clearly didn't go over so well.

I answered, clearing my thoughts, "It's very salvageable. In fact, I was calling to let you know he will be performing at the Flango Mango tonight."

"Flango Mango? No disrespect to you, Jayson, but I don't know what kind of poppers you've been sniffing if you think a singer who sold out stadiums is going to be performing at some sad shack of a venue."

"Are you done?" I asked, not wanting to entertain his sudden outburst. "If you want your client's image to be salvaged, as you say, then him performing at this small venue will have him and your label control the narrative. We cannot risk another screw up and him lashing out again. At least with Flango Mango, you show them a few hundreds and they'll gladly bark if you tell them too."

Silence fell between us, and I knew he was contemplating my words. No matter what he thought of my sudden plan, it was a good one and beneficial to Geo and the label.

"Fine," Marvin said as if had a choice in the matter. "I'll get the band to go down and create a set list with him."

"Speaking of set list, I informed Geo that if he wants to truly win back the audience, he has to write a new song that he will debut tonight."

"Are you out of your mind?! A new song? Even if we were to put him in the booth to record that song in the future, there's no guarantee anyone will buy it after what he said and did!" Marvin shouted into the phone.

Well, it seems this idea was inconvenient to him.

"I do love when people doubt my capabilities—" I stated, "This is all for you and the label. The audience will be told by him through the song that he is a scorned lover who didn't know how to hold onto his anger. The song he will be debuting will be a lover's revenge story. Everyone loves a good f-you song."

Once again, as if I was psychic, or because I'm good at my job, Marvin agreed with me, calling my idea the best one yet.

"I know. Just make sure you have him under control. Flipping out at Flango Mango could be a career ender for him."

"Got you, Jayson. And thanks again."

I hung up the phone and let out a sigh of relief. Now I can bask in the knowledge that my work for today was over.

I didn't have any clients scheduled so I could easily just go home and relax...ah who am I kidding? Relaxation is a word I barely know the definition of.

"Alrighty. Let's get some dinner and head home." I spoke out loud as I grabbed my purple jacket, placed it on, grabbed my phone, car and building keys and headed out the door of *Fame Fixer Inc.* Turning the lights to the office off, I closed the door and locked it. I looked out of the window in the hallway to see it was completely dark outside. I had forgotten how quickly it turns to night here in New Fran City. I walked down the steps of the building and heard my phone ring.

"Dammit! So much for my day ending early." I stopped walking and took my phone out to see the caller ID had '*Sal*' on it.

Walking down the steps, I answered the phone. "Hola, *sexy hombre mío*," I smiled, passing the second floor and continuing down the steps.

"Boots...wh...where...you?"

I ,frowned not sure why my phone was sounding as if either of us was going under a tunnel. "Sal, I can't hear you."

I pushed the lobby door open and was met by the cold winter wind, which made me shiver. I saw my purple Mini Cooper parked across the street and walked over to the curb.

"Boots! Where are you?" he asked. His tone was filled with fear.

"I'm heading home now. Why? Are you gonna pick me up?" I smirked.

"You are in danger! Get to safety now!"

"What the hell are you talking abou—"

BOOOOOOOOOOMMMMMMM!!!

.

.

.

Chapter 13

E<u>ight minutes earlier...</u>
     "Till Death Do Us Part"

Pseudocide...I honestly don't know what got me interested in choosing that as my fictitious career. I tried so many times to think of why I chose that or let alone, how the hell I— Salvatore Maldonado—came up with it.

Did I see a documentary about it? Or maybe read it in a book? No *sé*. But it definitely worked out to my advantage. Especially when it came to meeting Jayson. Or Boots, as I call him.

Boots is a nickname I gave to him because I noticed he wears boots in every season. Summer, fall, spring and winter. It's actually cute, one of the many things I love about him.

"Ah, love." I sighed, hearing the word come out of my mouth and realizing that I, stupidly and dangerously fell into that slimy pit of love. It almost cost me my life and career!

But I shouldn't dwell too much on the past, that's over with. I need to focus on the present and future, a future that I want to spend with Boots, although due to the current circumstances, I'm afraid that will not be coming into fruition sooner than I thought.

I turned off the television in my apartment and looked down at my phone. Every fiber of my being wanted to text Boots and ask if he was free for dinner. Of course, the dinner would be at a fancy restaurant and then maybe stopping off at an abandoned alleyway where he could give me a consensual blowjob.

The doorbell caused me to flinch, which was funny since I forgot I ordered food earlier.

I walked over to the door, unlocked and opened it, expecting to find the delivery man, but instead, standing on my doorstep was a man who looked like he was currently going through a midlife crisis. He had gray or silver hair that was slicked back and he reeked of cigar and alcohol. By his stench alone, someone would confuse him for a nearby hobo, but based on his Italian leather boots and designer clothes, this stranger was rich...or at least that's what he was presenting himself as. He wore a smile on his wrinkle free face and I noticed a red folder in his right hand. What the hell was this weirdo going to sell me now?

"Can I help you?" I asked.

"Why, I sure as hell hope you can. My name is Jordan Monroe and I am here to make all your dreams come true."

Hearing those words come out of his mouth made me flinch in horror. "No offense, but I don't bang old dudes."

"Ouch." he replied, clenching his chest, clearly showing me my words offended him. "No worries, I was actually referring to the divorce between Jayson and yourself. I have some very valuable information that can benefit you."

I looked at him, not in confusion, but more so out of curiosity on why he had Boots' name in his mouth. "How do you know about the divorce? Our lawyers have signed NDAs."

"Ah yes, well, when you dangle money in front of the right people they tend to sing like canaries."

"And a canary sang for you? What song did they sing?"

"How about you take a look and tell me for yourself?"

He handed me the folder. I was really hungry and the last thing I wanted was company.

I opened the folder to find two pictures of Jayson and Anthony. These appeared to have been taken without their knowledge. I turned the page and tried to read the document that followed, but the words were in Greek.

My eyes darted back to the man, whose name I already forgot and I asked, "What exactly am I looking at?"

The man was still smiling and replied, "Ah, that is the million-dollar question. We should talk about this in private. Especially since this information can make you a very rich man."

The last thing I wanted was to invite this man into my apartment, but he clearly has some very important information on Jayson and Anthony. I figured I would entertain him.

"Fine, but let's make it quick."

I placed the folder under my right arm and stepped aside, opening the door wider. He bowed his head, walked in and I closed the door behind him.

There wasn't any hallway in the loft, which is why I adored living here. Well, that and it was far away from people, or so I thought.

"So how much do you want for this information?" I asked, leaning against the counter of my kitchen, which was the first room anyone who enters is introduced to.

"Oh, you misheard me, Salvatore. I'm not here to blackmail you. I'm here to tell you what that folder contains so it can help you."

"Help me?" I asked, chuckling to myself. "Why the hell would you want to help me? You don't even know me."

"You're right about that. But you and I are closer than you think. We have one thing in common."

I watched as he sat on my sofa as if he was an invited guest. "We do? And what exactly is that?"

"Our disdain for one named Jayson Romero."

I inhaled deeply, doing my best not to show one ounce of anger I had for this man who kept on mentioning Boots' name.

"That folder you have contains everything you need to destroy Jayson. While you do so, I get to sit back and enjoy the show. Of course, that is if you don't want the five million dollar bounty someone put out on his life."

Hmm, this *abuelo bronceado dorado* seems to know about this bounty, maybe I should continue with this act.

I opened the folder again and turned the pages to find another round of pictures of Jayson, Anthony and a middle-aged Latin man who looked like he was a male model for GQ. He was wearing a very expensive designer suit and tie. But once again none of the words were in English.

"Unless you think I speak Greek, I have no idea what any of this means," I stated.

"Ah, so let me break it down for you, my young padawan." he said as he rose from the sofa and walked toward me.

I didn't get a chance to speak or let alone think when Jordan pulled the picture of the man in the designer suit out of my hand. "This is Javi Castillo. The most dangerous man in New York City, New Fran and even Chicago."

¡Nada de mierda, Sherlock!

"He is the head of the *Tribu de Aries.* An organized gang that puts the Cartel to shame."

"So, he's a wanted man?"

"You would think so. But not quite. Apparently, everyone is scared of him, including the police, FBI, mayors, governors, president, you name it. Why? Because he supplies these people with weapons, intel on foreign affairs, etc. But weirdly he never deals with drugs."

I nodded, not entirely sure what any of this had to do with why this man was here, but it made sense to him, so I let him continue on blabbing. Maybe he would finally get to the point?

"Now, you're probably asking what this has to do with anything, well, let me explain. Javi Castillo met a woman three decades ago named Samaya. She was an actress, notorious in Latin soap operas. It was love at first sight. They got married and had a kid, but then tragedy struck. On the eve of January 20th, 1993, Samaya killed herself after someone sent her a letter proving that her marriage to Javi was a fraud. It was a fraud because Javi was already married to someone else. This meant poor Samaya was the other woman. The revelation hurt her, it hurt her so much that she blew her brains out as her baby slept in the next room. Poor Javi was so depressed he couldn't handle raising his kid all by himself, so he ended up giving away his and Samaya's baby to her mother. A very famous realtor named Penelope Romero. He knew she would be the perfect one to raise his son away from the dark Romero family life."

"Okay." I added pressing pause on whatever the hell he was about to say next as he inhaled deeply. "And what does this have to do with me again?"

He let out a deep sigh, I guess I offended him with my question, "God, you are so dense. Jayson Romero is Javi and Samaya's son! His real name is Javier Romero Castillo Jr."

I let out a gasp. He gave me a nod as if he was proud of my reaction.

"But there's more to this story, sunshine. I'm sure you know Anthony Santos?"

Once again, I nodded, "Yeah that's his assistant. He was some drug dealer that Jayson took off the streets and gave him work legally."

The geezer began to slowly clap his hands as if I had just finished performing for him and he shook his head in awe of my words. "I have to admit, that son of a bitch is an amazing liar. He really contrived all of that information and you stupidly believed him?"

"Then who is he?" I asked, feeling my patience diminish.

"Javi was married to a woman named Rosita Cruz. They had a son named Anthony Hector Cruz Romero. He was only seven years old when his mother wrote a letter to Samaya, telling her the truth about Javi."

I felt my heart skip a beat, like I hear people talk about that happening, but I never believed them. Except at this moment, my heart literally skipped a beat because that's how upset and shocked I was!

Jordan was looking for a reaction from me. I could feel his eyes practically burning a hole through me. Huh, maybe I should act a bit more surprised.

I let out a gasp, "Wait, does Jayson know that he and Anthony are brothers?"

"Of course, he does!" the man stated, "Anthony was the one that found Jayson five years ago. I believe his presence was what caused dear old Penelope Romero to have a heart attack and die. But the jury is still out on that one."

I didn't have any words to say. Boots found this out around the time he and I were already dating. He knew all of this and didn't tell me anything. Did he not trust me?

"Why did Anthony decide to work with Jayson as his assistant?" Out of all the bullshit I heard, that was the only question that came out of my mouth.

Weirdly, it appears this geezer knew the answer as he started explaining, "Anthony was Javi 's right-hand man. He helped his father carry out kills while wearing this scary Day of the Dead mask that looked like a painted skull with black painted eyes, but no mouth. Which is why the streets dubbed him, *El hombre del saco silencioso*, which is Spanish for 'The Silent Boogeyman'. I'm talking about bloody kills. Men with their tongues ripped out, beheaded, castrated, and even eaten by mountain lions. I guess Anthony needed a break from all the bloodshed, so he decided to stay in New Fran, and his brother created a position for him. I dunno, my source in Greece didn't get much into that. He sadly passed away in a tragic car accident a few days ago."

The geezer smiled and continued, "But ain't that some mind blowing shit right there? But it also explains why no one has tried to claim the five million dollar bounty I put on Jayson 's pretty little head. Which is why I'm here talking to you. Sometimes you have to get a man to do men's work."

This bastard was the one that put a bounty on Boots' head?!

I cleared my throat and asked, "So what's your plan here? Are you going to tell the press?"

"Tell the press? Oh no. You and I both know how good Jayson is with manipulating them. He would paint himself as the victim or become some goddam martyr. No, you are going to hit him where it hurts. You are going to help me get his little black book full of every single client that he has in the city. Then you can take every penny he has."

"Every penny?" I chuckled in the old man's delusional face. "How much money do you think he has?"

I thought that question was a valid one, but I was wrong because he replied with, "Damn, he didn't even tell you he's loaded?"

"Loaded? What the hell are you talking about?"

"Wow. You may want to sit down for this."

I glared at him, not entertaining the notion that I'm going to take a seat in my own apartment until this man leaves.

I guess he noticed my glare because he continued, "You remember Jayson 's little abuela?"

I coiled at the question because white people speaking Spanish with their plain and unseasoned accent sounded weird.

"Yeah."

"Well apparently, she was loaded and she left Jayson a hell of an inheritance."

"How much?"

"Let's just say, he is part of the one percent. Oh, and Lois Grant, dear ol' Jayson's ex-boss, left him $980 million in her will." My heart began to beat heavily in my chest. There's no way Boots would keep something like this away from me and if he had, where the hell was he hiding the money?

I shook my head and ran my fingers through my hair in frustration. I really should get an acting award for my abilities to pretend to be so dumb and clueless.

As the man stood there like a goddamn *fea estatua,* I pretended to think, making sure my face matched the fake thoughts I was forcing myself to have. For example: *I should take that lying bastard for everything he's worth! Leave him penniless, rotting in the streets and show him how much of a better man I am than him.*

"And what do you gain out of all this?" I asked my unwanted guest.

"His downfall, for starters. You see, I've been struggling to open my own public relations agency and right now, Jayson is the hottest thing. He's taking all the big- name clients, well not all the huge names, as another crisis manager named Laurel Quinn is still alive and kicking. But with Jayson out of the picture and with his black book of clients in my possession, I can become a very powerful man."

"So, it's an ego trip you're after?"

He rubbed his chin and nodded. "I guess you can say it is. Laurel Quinn is an old woman, all I have to do is flash a few millions in her face and she'll fly the coop to Mexico or wherever the hell women retire to nowadays." The man stopped speaking and he looked down at the watch on his right wrist. "Well, I gotta head out. I have a date with this fine ass model. Word on the street is, she'll do anything for a quick buck."

I nodded and made my way into the kitchen as the geezer headed straight toward the door.

"One more thing," I added, "Your source was misinformed about Anthony Santos. He has never been known as *el hombre del saco silencioso*."

"What are you talking about?"

"Well, it's true Javi is a dangerous man, but it's not because he kills people. It's because he knows every single secret of the rich and powerful. He was never the type to get his hands dirty. History did speak of his son being a cold-blooded killer, which is exactly what Anthony is. But the real killer. The real person who got their hands dirty, who tortured, maimed, decapitated, and put the heads of Javi's enemies on pikes for their families to see when they came home from a soccer game, wasn't Anthony."

I quickly grabbed a cast iron skillet that I had left on the stove and walked up to him as his back was turned to me, with pleasure and disdain in my eyes.

"The Silent Boogeyman the world is so scared of…is *me*!" I growled. I hit him over the head and he fell to the ground, dropping the phone right next to him.

"What the f-?!" he yelled out as he touched the back of his head and realized he was bleeding. "I'm going to sue your ass!" he stated.

"Alexa, play my workout playlist." I stated and within a second the sound of house music blasted throughout the loft.

"What the hell do you think you're doin—ah!"

I hit him again and again.

I felt his warm blood splatter onto my shirt, then onto my face as I continued to smash his head in with the skillet. The same skillet Boots brought me the first morning he stood at my apartment. He said my original skillet was rusted and needed to be cleansed of any bad aura from my exes.

A smile spread across my face as I remembered the first time Boots and I kissed.

Blam!

The first time we made love.

Blam!

The first time he moaned my name.

Blam!

The first time he said that he loved me.

Blam!

The night I proposed to him.

Blam!

Our wedding night!

Blam!

The reason why I let him go.

Blam!

Blam!

Blam!

I dropped the skillet onto the floor and looked down to see Jordan Monroe dead. His face was unrecognizable. Blood was all over my hands, shirt, the wall, the wooden floors...everywhere!

My eyes darted to the cellphone on the ground which laid in a pool of Jordan's blood.

I picked it up to see the screen had the text of the bounty he placed on Boots' head. Dumbass didn't even try to hide the fact or let alone lock the screen with a password.

Without much thinking I texted, "The contract is canceled!"

Placing the blood covered phone in my back pocket, I backed away slowly and walked into the bathroom. I looked into the mirror to see a broken man staring right back at me.

Some of his blood was on my face, as if it was his last second of mocking me. I quickly washed it off and my mind began to run amok trying to figure out my next move.

I decided to call an old friend who could help me with this. "Yo, it's Anthony." the voice answered from the other line. "Hey Ant. It's Salvatore." I replied calmly.

"Why are you calling me?"

"I need your help."

Anthony chuckled on the other line, "Man, I don't know what kind of drugs you're on but I ain't helping you with sh—"

I decided not to mention everything over the phone, so instead I recited a quote I heard many years ago, one that I knew he would recognize almost immediately. *"Cuando mi papá no me tomó de la mano, me cubrió la espalda."* (When my dad did not hold my hand, he had my back.).

"Wait...that's my dad's quote. How did you—"

"No time to explain. I'll send you the address here and Anthony? Bring your cleaning gear." I hung up the phone, texted my address to him and let out a sigh, staring at the dead man in my apartment. Really wishing my food got here sooner because I'm starving even more now.

••••

A FEW MOMENTS LATER:

I lost track of time once I let Anthony inside to work his magic. Normally whenever I kill, I prop up the body as a message for the family and loved ones of the victim to find...but this time it was different. Different because I wasn't hired to kill Jordan and quite frankly, I doubt he had anyone that cared if he was missing.

As Anthony wrapped up the body, I took a shower to wash away the blood from my face and hair. While I stood naked under the running hot water, I closed my eyes, remembering the first time I laid eyes on Boots at that *aburrido como la mierda* party.

The way I was only supposed to observe him from a distance, yet I found myself drawn to him. Like he was the flame of purity, sweetness and happiness and I was the *maldita polilla* (fucking moth)! Every day after that, I found myself falling for him. His infectious laugh, his smile, his cute little sneezes that reminded me of a kitten. Loving how sweet he tasted. How soft his bare skin always was, how tight his full lips would get around my dick, and even how he would moan whenever I hit his spot, causing his body to shake uncontrollably after, as if he just rode the world's most dangerous roller coaster.

I finished up in the shower, dried off, put on my briefs, jeans and walked out of the bathroom with my hair still wet. I saw Anthony sitting on my sofa, taking a sip of beer and swallowing it down. "Hope you don't mind. I couldn't help myself."

"Nah, it's cool. I owe you."

He nodded, "Jordan's body is in the trunk of my car. I'll take him to the cliffs in a few."

When Anthony arrived here, I told him everything. About who I really was, about why I was at the party the night Boots and I met and even why I killed Jordan. I didn't give him much time to ask me follow up questions because I went to shower, letting him get to work on cleaning the mess I made. Clearly, from his demeanor he had a lot on his mind.

"Okay." I began, sitting on the recliner across from him. "Ask me whatever you wanna ask me."

He placed the beer on the coffee table and rubbed his forehead. "Well first off, did my dad send you here after he found out I was coming to meet Romero five years ago?"

That was a question that I'm sure was weighing heavy on his heart as he seemed so proud of himself to finally ask that and to probably get an answer to that question.

"No. He sent me to stop you. Once your mother told him she told you all about Samaya and the affair, he feared you would find Boots—I mean Jayson —and kill him. Once I saw you didn't, you just developed some weird ass family relationship as if you knew each other for years, I figured he was safe. *But el jefe,* your dad, wanted me to stay for another week...until I ended up being caught by Boots and then ultimately falling for him."

"Dude, you're *el hombre del saco silencioso.* I have heard stories about you all throughout the streets. Every assassin knows not to mess with you. I was starting to think you were a myth...yet here you were married to my brother the whole time!" Anthony shook his head in disbelief or pride, I don't really know. His tone didn't match the smile he had on his face. "Does Romero know?"

I shook my head slowly, "No. I know I need to tell him and I promise I will tonight. It just hasn't really been smooth sailing for him and I ever since we met."

Anthony sat up on the sofa and leaned forward, spreading his legs as if he was about to tell me a secret or something. "My father hired you to watch him and you fell in love with him. You honestly thought it would be smooth sailing?"

"Of course not! I knew there would be issues and I explained it to *el jefe* but he didn't want to hear it. He thought I betrayed him or I was using his son in some sick scheme to get revenge on him."

"And you weren't?"

I once again shook my head, "Believe me Anthony, I love your brother. I would do anything for him. Hell, I just murdered someone for him!"

I mean, if that isn't any indication on how much I love Boots, then I have no idea what could be.

Anthony gave me a nod and leaned back into the sofa, grabbing the beer and taking another sip.

I waited for him to swallow it before he asked, "Did Jordan tell you where he got the information from?"

"Kind of. He just told me that a person with a bone to pick with the family gave him all the intel. He didn't give any names, but it won't be hard to retrace his steps. A man like Jordan doesn't really have genuine friends."

"Only Oliver Morales." Anthony calmly said, causing me to look at him weirdly.

"The P.I who was killed in a car crash?"

Once again, he nodded, "Yeah, I had my suspicions about him when he came over the office trying to look at old security footage. He claimed there were car thefts around the neighborhood, but I know Sainero Rowe like the back of my hand. There were no car thefts. I followed him home, noticed he stopped off at a local gun shop, so I took him out by popping two of his tires with my gun as he sped down the freeway, he lost control and blam! *El bastardo* died on the spot."

I had to admire Anthony and his tactics. Sure, I wouldn't have made him die in a fiery crash like an amateur. I would've caught him when he was jogging or heading somewhere, then popped three caps into both of his knees and basked in his painful cries.

But who am I to judge? I stupidly killed a man with a damn skillet making a mess, ruining my hardwood floors and dirtying my jeans.

Anthony cleared his throat, "And what about the contract?"

"All Jordan. He came to me as a last resort because no one was biting at the bounty he put out."

Anthony was about to take another sip and he paused to look at me with a smirk, "Was no one biting because of you or because of my father?"

I gave him a sly grin, "You nailed it. But it doesn't matter, he never logged out of the site. So, I was able to cancel it." Anthony and I exchanged looks as we heard a cell phone ring. It was coming from Jordan's phone, which I placed on the counter, minutes ago.

I looked at the screen to see it was a timer and apparently the timer hit the one- minute mark.

"What the hell is he timing?" Anthony asked, probably looking over my shoulder.

"I don't know, but we need to get to Boots now."

"Let's go!" Anthony said, opening the door, "I'll drive."

"No! I'll head to Boots, you get rid of Jordan's body. Trust me, I got this."

I took my phone out and quickly called Boots, grabbing my black leather jacket and following the eldest Romero son out of my apartment.

"*Hola...hombre...mío.*" He answered as I descended the steps, forgetting that the reception in the staircase was horrible. The building was built sometime in the 1880s, although the staircase is on the side of the warehouse leading into the alleyway, for some odd reason the reception was horrible.

"Boots, where are you?"

"Sal...can't hear you."

I jumped off the last step as Anthony started his car. I got into my car, my heart racing. "Boots, where are you?" I repeated again as the static noise went down.

"I'm heading home now. Why? Are you gonna pick me up?"

"You are in danger! Get to safety now!"

"What the hell are you talking abou—"

Booooooommmm!

"Boots?! Boots?!"

The phone went dead and I no longer heard the static, the sound of the wind or Boots' voice...Just silence.

Chapter 14

The sound of sirens filled the usual busy street of Sainero Rowe. Cars were no longer honking because the police were directing traffic as the firefighters were finally able to fan the flames of what used to be my purple Mini Cooper.

I thanked God that the EMT workers, police officers and firefighters made a barrier, blocking the paparazzi and news reporters from taking pictures of me. They didn't have to, but considering the situation and who I was, I understood why they did it. The last thing I needed was the paparazzi and the news plastering my face on the twelve, four, five, six, ten and eleven o'clock news.

"Hello?" a woman's voice broke me out of my daydream and she snapped her fingers.

I blinked.

"Huh? Sorry." I forgot that I was sitting in the back of an ambulance with the EMT asking me questions about what day it was, who the president was and if I could count how many fingers she had up.

"What's your name?" she asked, not because she didn't know but rather to see if I knew.

"Jayson Romero," I replied, she nodded and smiled.

"Alright it looks like you didn't suffer any head injuries, which is amazing. Considering the impact of the blast, you got lucky. The detectives finished questioning you so we can take you to the nearest hospital or..."

"Boots?" I heard Salvatore's voice and I looked to find him walking toward me.

I smiled and jumped out of the ambulance, hugging him tightly.

"Are you okay?" he asked, to which I just gave a nod. I tried everything not to cry, but the tears were coming out of my closed eyelids as if it was a ceiling leak being sealed up with Scotch tape.

When the car's explosion caused me to fall back, I laid motionless while staring up at the black sky. As that happened, I swear on all that is holy, I heard Salvatore's voice in my head telling me a cheesy dad joke.

As I laid there in shock, I could only think about the last time he held me. How he dug his nails in my skin as he thrusted his hips until his erect length hit my spot, bringing us to relief. Then when he caressed my legs as we binge watched some boring show, I felt myself melt all over again.

And now seeing him here...is this a sign from the universe or some hippy deity?

I pulled away from him slowly and he grabbed my face with both his hands, which made me flinch a little. I forgot there was a piece of debris from the explosion which smacked me across my right cheek. While I clearly forgot, the painful sensation that emitted from the cheek due to Sal's touch was a huge reminder.

"Sorry." he apologized when I flinched, but I told him not to worry about it.

He looked at the EMT worker and then back at me, "*¿Puedes ir a casa o quieren que vayas al hospital?*" (Are you able to go home or do they want you to go to the hospital?)

I rolled my eyes, "*Me lo dejan a mí. Pero me siento bien. Solo quiero irme a casa.*" (They're leaving it up to me. But I feel fine. I just want to go home).

He nodded, wrapped his arm around my waist and guided me away from the chaos that was now taking over Sainero Rowe.

The explosion didn't do any damage to the building—thankfully—but my car is gone.

The car wasn't just a car. It was my abuela's, and she left it to me in her will, and seeing it blown up into pieces made me feel like she died all over again.

Then again, if she was alive right now, she would tell me

"Un coche es un elemento materialista. Estás vivo, respirando y eso es más importante que algo fabricado en England." Which translates to: "A car is a materialistic item. You're alive, breathing, and that's more important than something that was manufactured in England."

I decided to clear my mind of the memories I've had with my car and focus on the positive, getting home, showering and trying to make sense of what the hell happened, but Salvatore stopped walking and he looked at me with a somber expression on his face. "What's going on? Why do you look the way you did when you found out that Cuban rapper Pablo G is actually Dominican?"

He inhaled and then exhaled, grabbing my right hand, "Boots, we need to talk."

"Are you going to divorce me again?" I asked jokingly, hoping to at least get a chuckle from him, instead he just looked at me, making me worry even more.

"I know all about you and Anthony being brothers. And I know your father is Javi Castillo."

My heart sank to my stomach and is now being destroyed by the stomach acid—okay, probably a bad metaphor, but I'm literally in shock—and the only thing I could do to make this go my way was to think of a lie.

I shook my head and smiled, "That's a crazy accusation and imagination you have. No wonder why I fell in love with you."

"Jordan Monroe told me. He's the one that put the bounty out on you."

I felt anger explode inside of me after hearing Salvatore tell me that. The same man that came to my office asking about working for me was the same one that wanted me dead?

"I'm going to kill him." I replied, shaking my head.

"Yeah, I kinda beat you to it."

Those words caused me to look at him once again in confusion, however, this time I was more worried about what he said as he wasn't smirking or let alone joking.

"What are you talking about?"

Salvatore nodded as if I asked if he enjoyed killing Jordan, because strangely, he didn't show any signs of remorse on his face. That was beginning to worry me. "You're going to have to explain all of this to me because right now I am confused as hell."

"Alright. Jordan visited my apartment and told me he wanted to bring you down. He had a folder which contained everything on you and Anthony being brothers and Javi being your father. I was confused at first, but he wanted me to steal your black book with all your client's information in it."

Of course! That son of a bitch was always looking for an easy way to get what he wanted. Never once did Jordan work hard to achieve something meaningful. Even now, he put a bounty on my head to have me killed and then tried to entice my ex-husband to work with him? I hope he's right now rotting in hell.

This night was really starting to drive me insane. Although my mind was reeling from the information I just learned, I looked at Salvatore to try and understand why he did what he did.

Most people who kill for the first time would feel a sense of guilt because they took a life, but not Sal. His tone was filled with pride and accomplishment as if this was on his vision board when he was younger.

"So, because of that you decided to kill him? Why didn't you just come to me? I would've handled it my own way. The *right* way."

"Boots, me killing him was the only way. He knew too much and I had to make sure he didn't tell anyone else."

I looked at Sal, not sure where this new attitude was coming from. It was assertive and protective, I swear I've ever seen it before on him.

Before I could ask him what he did with the body, he interrupted me, "I know you're probably in shock, but there's more to this. Have you heard of *el hombre del saco silencioso*?"

"Yes, of course. The Silent Boogeyman was my father's right-hand man. No one had ever seen his face because he wears this scary looking Mexican Macho Mula mask that resembles a monster. Why?"

"Well...I'm him."

I remained silent and just stared blankly at him, wondering if I was currently suffering from a concussion. The way I landed after my car exploded, I protected my head, but I felt with all this information that I was definitely suffering from some kind of hallucination. There is no way that my ex-husband could possibly be my father's hitman...there's no way.

mouth."There's no way," I said, not believing one word out of his.

He gave me a nod and slowly reached in the inside of his black leather jacket causing me to step back slowly. "I'm not going to hurt you." He pulled out a cell phone and unlocked it.

"Part of my contract with *el jefe* is to kill anyone he hires me to and to show proof of it. In doing so, I take pictures of them to prove they're dead. Would you like to see some?"

"God, no!" I quickly retorted, never wanting to see anyone that he killed. Was he smoking some kind of crack to assume I would be open to seeing anything that gruesome?

"Boots." He grabbed my hands again and gazed into my eyes, "I am telling you the truth. *El jefe* hired me to watch over you. He knew you still living in New Fran City would cause problems because of the enemies he's made in the past. So, he wanted you to have a protector. Unfortunately, I was unaware that Anthony would be that protector for you. Even then, my cover was blown at that party when you spotted me and we spoke. I fell in love with you Boots, something I had never done with anyone. *El jefe* didn't know, but when he did find out he wanted us to divorce. I did that to make sure we were good. Boots, he gave me the okay. That's why I came back. Once we found out about the bounty, he put me on the first flight here."

I shook my head, feeling as if it was being filled with too much information. Leaving no room for my brain to digest all this and no time for me to take all of it into consideration.

"So, you being a pseudocode agent for the government was a lie?"

He nodded.

"And all those people you claimed you had to help fake their deaths...were really people you killed with your bare hands?"

Once again, he nodded, "Some I did, others I shot with my silencer and some I pushed off the roof to make it look like suicide. But yes, ideally it was all real and all the people *el jefe* wanted me to murder."

"Speaking of *el jefe*, where is my father? I've seen the news. He escaped prison with two men. Where are they hiding?"

I expected Sal to change the subject or better yet, to wrap his arms around my waist and kiss me to make me forget all about what I asked—as he would normally do whenever we would get into small arguments—but instead he looked back down at his phone.

He pressed a button and handed it to me. "Here."

"What the hell?"

"Ask him all you need to."

Him? I took the phone and placed it on my right ear. "Hello?" I asked, feeling like a moron not knowing who the hell I was talking to.

"*Hola hijo.*" The voice on the other line sent chills down my spine.

I haven't heard this voice in so long. Just in distant memories in my brain whenever I would be sleeping.

"Dad?" I gasped, looking at Sal, who leaned against his car.

"*Sé que ha pasado un tiempo y por eso lo siento. Pero quiero que sepas que nunca dejé de cuidarte.*" (I know it's been a while and for that I'm sorry. But I want you to know, I never stopped looking after you.).

"*¿Tú o tu mano derecha aquí? El maldito coco silencioso.*" (You or your right-hand here? The freaking Silent Boogeyman.) I retorted, glaring at Sal.

"I don't have much time to talk, Jayson. But I am glad to see and hear you are doing fine. I know that Salvatore has your back and for that I will be making sure he serves the *Tribu de Aries* by protecting you."

"I don't need a bodyguard! I've been doing fine before some *viejo culo chico blanco* ordered a hit out on me to try and steal my client list. I assure you, I will be fine."

There were a few seconds of silence on the other line, I have no idea where my father could be located, but wherever he was, there was no background noise, just pure silence. "Do you remember the last thing I told you before you left with your *abuela* to New Fran City?"

Honestly? No. I was roughly around one when that happened. I remember being confused as to why my mom wasn't coming with us, because at that age I didn't know anything about death or let alone the crap she went through— crap that *he* put her through. Those were things I learned about later in life.

I guess he took my silence for a "No" as he continued.

"I told you, No *importa dónde termines en la vida. Siempre seré tu padre y aunque la cagué, la arreglaré y recuperaré el tiempo perdido.*" (No matter where you end up in life. I will always be your father and although I screwed up, I will fix it and make up for the time lost.)

While it made sense during the timing, I didn't think it would mean twenty-five years later he would break out of a prison—that I'm still not sure how he ended up there to begin with—to go into hiding just to make his way toward me. That sounded like an idiotic plan and one that I doubt, a man who literally runs the Spanish Mafia would be stupid enough to make.

"But Dad, you can't come to New Fran City for obvious reasons."

"I know *hijo*, that's why I'll be laying low. I have a plan and sadly, I won't be able to see you until a few months, but trust me. Everything will work out and then you, me and Anthony will be reunited again."

That plan sounded amazing, in his own head I'm sure, but there was a lot of anger that Anthony had buried when he found me five years ago. He didn't think his father had originally cheated on his mother or let alone had another kid, but all that subsided once he got to know me. Then we started to get along like brothers do. He never once told me if he had visited our dad in prison, or wrote to him at least to show how angry he was.

None of that happened.

I didn't want to waste whatever few seconds I had with my dad on the phone, asking about him and Anthony's relationship, so I decided to instead focus on the two men my dad escaped prison with.

I asked him about them and all he said was, "In due time you'll know them. Now put Salvatore back on the phone."

"Alright."

"Listen Jayson ...I love you and happy birthday."

I smiled, well at least tried to, because my face was still in pain, and I replied, "Thank you and I love you too, Dad."

I handed the phone back to Salvatore and I walked around the car, opened the passenger door and slowly got in. Salvatore took the phone and began to talk to my father as he slowly closed the passenger door once I was fully inside of the car.

I leaned my head against the window and closed my eyes. This night has been one crazy ass ride.

One that I hope will not get crazier.

Chapter 15

<u>**January 20, 2023:**</u>

Yesterday felt like a fever dream. From my car exploding, to the confession of Sal knowing about Anthony, myself and my father. Then to his confession about being a very dangerous killer, I honestly woke up thinking it was all a bad dream. Until I felt my back hurt and realized the explosion was real.

I looked to my right to find Sal sleeping on a recliner he brought in from the living room. He was worried about me, so he wanted to watch me sleep, and I guess he thought someone would have the balls to break in so he kept his SIG Sauer Mosquito gun on his lap.

I smiled and got off the bed slowly, my body felt like I got hit by a freight train or like Piper, Phoebe and Paige, after they were thrown like rag dolls on every episode of *Charmed*.

I walked into the bathroom and turned the lights on to look at my reflection. The cut on my forehead was small, the way the EMT made it seem when she was putting on a long band aid, made me think it was much worse.

The bruise on my face wasn't as bad as it looked last night. Maybe I'm a fast healer.

I inhaled and exhaled deeply, letting out a sigh filled with relief, and for the first time on this day...appreciation for having survived another year. "Happy birthday."

"Hey, Boots." I heard Sal say as he walked into the bathroom slowly. "How are you feeling?" I looked at his reflection in the mirror and smiled, "Considering everything...I'm doing well. And thank you."

The confusion on his face was priceless. He looked as if I had just told him my twin brother was coming over for dinner or something. "Thank you for what?"

"For staying over. For being honest with me. I don't know, for accepting me and my crazy ass family for starters? Most guys would be running for the hills by now."

Sal let out a chuckle and shook his head, "Are you kidding me? I told you I killed people for your father and you still let me stay over. That in itself, is a miracle."

As much as I wanted to continue thanking him for never leaving my side, I needed to take a shower before Anthony came with my morning coffee and a lemon poppy seed muffin—a birthday tradition. I took off my shirt and underwear, turning the warm water on in the shower.

I decided to counter whatever question Sal was going to ask about my wellbeing by wrapping my arms around the back of his neck as the steam from the shower started to fill the bathroom.

"Do you wanna continue asking me about last night's near-death experience or do you want to give me an early birthday pounding in the shower?"

I slowly licked his lips and he smirked at me.

"Shit, when you put it like that." He leaned down to kiss my lips softly and I helped him take off his tank top, then his underwear, and he picked me up from the floor.

My body still ached, but none of that mattered right now.

Sal carried me into the shower and closed the glass door behind us. I pulled the small lever up, causing the shower head to turn on.

As we kissed under the water, I felt just like I did on our honeymoon. The feeling that I could conquer the world with the one man that I was in love with by my side. As he kissed me passionately, I felt his heart beat faster in his chest, the love we felt was still there and it got even more powerful when all of our secrets were exposed.

Sure, I would've loved to tell him myself as I'm sure he would've loved to tell me how he's been working for my father for the past ten years, but there was a reason why our secrets came out and I couldn't be any more happier, and I honestly wouldn't have it any other way.

Sal put me down so my feet touched the floor and he turned me around, pressing me up against the cold tiled wall of the shower.

I spread myself, giving him a clear pathway into my entrance. I felt his hand on my stomach and without any hesitation he slowly pushed the swollen head of his length inside of me. My moan was soon quieted when I heard him say, "Marry me again."

Of course, being in a trance with him pushing every inch of himself further inside of me, I looked over my shoulder at him. "What?"

"We're meant for each other. We have survived this long. Marry me."

"But what about my dad?"

"He gave me his blessing the second he told me to come down here."

The thoughts of Salvatore and I getting remarried started to flood my brain as I started to bounce back and forth on his length, the applause of my butt cheeks echoing through the steamy shower.

Sure, being married to Sal was amazing. We were working all throughout the week, and on the weekends, we would go to museums, flea markets, etc., but things were different then.

We—although we loved each other more than anything— were living a lie! We were hiding secrets from one another, secrets we feared would cause the other to run...but that was the past, now those dark secrets we feared would be the end of us, are now out in the light.

"You better get me a new ring," I replied, shivering as he quickened his pace. The second his member hit my prostate I started to whimper. He was the only man that knew how to make love to me without any guidance. His length was like the key God created to unlock the pleasures of my body. Pleasures that I didn't know I had until him. And while I tried to think of reasons why remarrying him was a mistake, I couldn't see myself with anyone else.

Who the hell has the time to start over? Not only that, but to start over and come out to that future partner about me being the result of an affair my mom had with the leader of the Spanish Mafia? Oy!

Sal smirked and held my throat, but not too tightly, it was just to hold me in place. I dropped my head back as he started to thrust in and out, "I'll get you whatever kind of ring you want."

I tried to answer, but because our bodies were so in sync we both released at the same time. Our orgasms echoed throughout the bathroom and probably the entire apartment.

As the hot water rained down our bodies and we panted to catch our breaths, I smiled, realizing this was the perfect start of my birthday; a day that I always thought was cursed.

A day that I dreaded more than anything in these past few years and here I was with my ex-husband—well soon to be husband again.

As my entrance tightened around his softening length, he pulled out slowly and chuckled in my ear, "Happy birthday, Boots."

A smile spread across my face and I kissed his lips passionately and deeply.

I heard the doorbell ring and I knew that was Anthony with my birthday breakfast, but I didn't want to let Sal go.

For the first time in a long time, I was happy on my birthday.

Now I just have to get through the next 365 days, unsure what type of scandals my clients will get into.

Unsure of who else might try to kill me.

And unsure of what secrets Hollywood 2.0 will want me to hide from the world.

Whatever my future holds, I will be there, facing it with my husband and brother by my sides.

Fixer Fame Inc and Jayson Romero will *never* die.

• • • •

THE END